AN ELI CARVER SUPERNATURAL THRILLER

GHOST RECALL

ALAN BAXTER

OTHER BOOKS BY ALAN BAXTER

GHOST RECALL
ISBN-13: 978-1-950569-08-3
Grey Matter Press First Trade Paperback Edition - December 2021

Copyright © 2021 Alan Baxter
Cover/Book Design Copyright © 2021 Grey Matter Press
Cover Font Design Copyright © 2021 Sabercore Art
Edited by Anthony Rivera

GREY MATTER
P R E S S

CHICAGO

Grey Matter Press
greymatterpress.com

Grey Matter Press on Facebook
facebook.com/greymatterpress

AN ELI CARVER SUPERNATURAL THRILLER

GHOST RECALL

ALAN BAXTER

ONE

TROUBLE FINDS ME LIKE FLIES FIND SHIT. Then again, I do like to see a motherfucker's tooth spinning through the air, his lip spraying blood like a split hose jetting water. Gonna have to get these knuckles cleaned up though. The germs people have in their mouth would make you sick to think about, and knuckles always get opened up by a motherfucker's teeth, and often end up infected. That's a concern for later though. I was aiming for his nose, but we can't always have what we want.

"Duck," Michael Privedi says.

I don't pause to think about why the ghost of my dead friend would say that, I simply comply. A piece of splintered two-by-four whistles over where my head was a fraction of a second before. I use my downward momentum to plant my hands and bring my leg around, sweeping the shithead's feet right out. He up-ends and hits the asphalt of the dirty alley on his back with a rush of escaping air and a *thock!* as the back of his head connects and he's out. Always an advantage of hard ground.

Burst Lip Asshole has regained his composure and found a new measure of anger, and his two mates are less surprised and more ready now. Four on one was tough going, now it's three on one and they're spread out wide across the alley, planning to paste me. Still tough going then.

"You are truly boned now, cocheese," the ghost of Dwight Ramsey says, blood trickling down his nose from the bullet hole between his eyes.

Oh, good. The gang's all here. Officer Graney, his throat ruined by the bullet I put through it and more scarlet blooms on the chest of his police shirt, is standing beside Dwight, ready to enjoy the show. Sylvester Barclay is leaning against the wall farther away, organs glistening where I blasted a shotgun shell through his chest, smoking his ubiquitous joint. Blue smoke curls out of his wide-open ribcage. Michael is somewhere behind me. Only Alvin Crake is missing, but I'm sure he's here somewhere. Ghosts of the bastards I killed. Well, five of the many. I still don't know why only these five. Now is not the time to think about it.

Michael strolls around behind the goons, the explosion of bone and brains where his ear used to be reflecting a streetlight at the end of the alley. He's the only kill I really regret, but he gave me no choice. "Better focus, dickhead," he says.

He's right.

"Gonna fucking kill you," Burst Lip Asshole says. Well, slurs.

They advance in a line, the other two fanning ahead and wide of Burst Lip, planning to flank me. I wish I had my guns on me, but I've got out of the habit of carrying them. Getting complacent. Now is not the time to think about that either.

Rule one of fighting multiple opponents: hit the leader first, to undermine the confidence of his lackeys. I assume Burst Lip Asshole is the boss here. Rule two of fighting multiple opponents: make space. Here I go, rules one and two together.

Instead of backing up like they expect, I rush Burst Lip. His hands are up, he thinks he's ready for me, but I sidestep at the last second and stiff-arm him, collecting one arm and his face as his punch finds only air. My forearm, hard as wood from a lot of training, slams him backwards. At the same moment I tuck my hip, lift my right knee and power out a kick into the ribs of the goon on that side. He folds up over my foot, crying out in pain, but I'm already planting that foot back on the ground and pivoting, bringing my other hand around in a tight hook that connects with beautiful solidity right behind Burst Lip's ear. He grunts and staggers forward, as good as out. His body just hasn't realized yet. The third goon, finding himself too far away, tries to close the distance and runs right into my front kick.

A good front kick is none of this snapping bullshit so many dojos try to teach. It's knee up high and drive out, the same as if you were trying to kick down a door. One of the most under-rated techniques in any kind of fighting. I hear at least three of the dude's ribs snap under my foot and he clutches himself and collapses, howling in high-pitched agony, which is a strange noise when most of the breath has already left a body.

I turn one-eighty and punch the other goon back into the wall just as he's trying to stand up from my side kick and he drops like a sack of bolts.

Burst Lip Asshole has fallen to his knees, one hand pressed to the back of his head where I punched him. It must hurt because my knuckles are singing with pain. I hope my hand isn't broken, but it could be. You don't often get to hit some fucker's skull with all your strength and not break something. But my hands are pretty well conditioned to this type of activity, so I might be lucky.

"Ah, for fuck's sake," Dwight says, disappointed once again.

I walk around in front of Burst Lip Asshole and grab a fistful of his jacket, haul him up to look at me. "Why the fuck are you shitstains following me?"

"Lotta money on you," he says, sounding confused. He's punch-drunk, that weird state of not actually knocked out, but also not really conscious. His friends are starting to groan and I keep an eye on them, just in case anyone pulls a piece. I need to move along, this is a busy town and people are walking past the alley in droves. Someone will look in soon and it might be a cop.

"Cops are the least of your worries," Officer Graney says, voice harsh because he doesn't really have a throat to speak of. I don't understand how he talks at all, but then again, he is dead, so what rules should apply? Like Sly getting high with no lungs.

"That's it?" I ask. "Money?"

"Saw you cash out, leave the casino."

"That's my girlfriend's money. You think I'd just let you take it?" Bridget is a hell of a gambler, she's got Las Vegas twisted around her finger, playing all the casinos. Enough to get rich, but not enough to notice. Not yet. I cash up for her a couple of times a night, stash the money in a safe at our rented apartment. Every couple of days I take about half the winnings to the bank, but keep the rest loose. Avoid a little government attention, maybe. It's a good life, or it has been for the last few months. I think maybe we're both getting bored. Itchy feet.

"Didn't think you'd have a choice," Burst Lip says. "Four on one."

"Unlucky for you." I pop him, a short, fast jab across the point of the chin and he sags like an empty wineskin. I turn to leave, then pause. A quick search of the four turns up phones, about six hundred bucks in cash, and two 9mm automatics. Seems like poetic justice to me. I leave their cell phones, too much trouble to get rid of these days. Leave the guns too, who knows the history of those irons. Then I see a nice signet ring on Burst Lip's index finger. Thick and heavy, got to be a fair amount of gold in that. It has a black stone on top, maybe onyx, with a strange symbol carved into it. Whatever, the gold alone is probably worth more than the cash I took. His ring goes into my jeans pocket, the guns go into a dumpster, and I add the cash to Bridget's winnings to put in the safe for later. We've got a good amount put away. Maybe it's time we started thinking about a holiday.

Six months, she told me, to get cashed up. Then take a break and live large for a while. When the money starts running out, find a new casino and start over. Maybe Monaco, she said. Sounds pretty sweet. It's only been three months and we're already loaded. I can't see us hanging out here another three. But right now, as long as I get to hang out with her, I'm happy. The money is good, the lifestyle is enviable, and the sex is out of this world. And she's smart and funny and sassy. For the first time, the pain of the wound Caitlyn and Scotty left in me is a little bit dulled. It'll never go away, but with Bridget around it's easier to live with.

Given my life up until now, I guess I don't really deserve it, but I've been through a lot of shit. I'll take the win, for as long as it lasts. Nothing lasts forever, after all. But this? With Bridget? Feels like it might.

"Why the hell you tell him about the fucker what snuck up behind?" Dwight says.

"Yeah, why?" Alvin Crake says, bullet hole glistening in his forehead. So, there he is.

Of course, no matter how well things might be going, there's always these assholes. I turn off the main street, foot traffic thins considerably, and the five of them are walking with me like we're some kind of gang.

"Habit, I guess," Michael says.

"Would have been perfect if some fucking losers killed him in a dirty alley," Sly says, blowing out a cloud of bluish smoke. "He deserves an ignominious end."

"An igno what now?" Dwight says. "Speak fucking English."

Sly laughs, even I can't help cracking a smile at Dwight's racist ignorance. Then again, to be as hatefully racist as Dwight, you have to be dumb as a brick.

"Why *did* you save him?" Graney asks Michael. "It's been so quiet for so long, this was the first chance we've had in ages to let him get hurt."

It's true. Since we left New York, I've barely had a raised word with anyone. Come to think of it, just now is the first fight I've had since the gun battle at the Vesuvius Lounge in Newark. It's been the longest peaceful period of my life that I recall. Funny I hadn't even noticed. Even these ghosts have been more distant in that time, only showing up now and then to harass me for the sport of it.

"What do you think happens when he does?" Michael asks.

Graney frowns. "Does what?"

"Gets hurt. Or even dies. What then?"

I turn into our building, trot upstairs to the third floor and unlock the apartment. The ghosts are already inside, time and space seem a little more flexible to them than the living. They sit around the front room, staring at each other. Part of me knows what Michael's getting at. It's something I've thought about over the last few months. Seems tonight's fight has stirred it up in Michael too. Of course, what I think and what they think is the same, isn't it? Or not? That's something else I've been ruminating on since New York. I still can't be sure all our minds aren't just my mind, still fractured from grief and stress. But I doubt it more by the day. Now I'm inside, I chance talking to them.

"Papa Night, huh?"

They turn to stare at me. Michael nods. "It's something to consider," he says.

Duck.

How did I know to duck back there? Did I sense the guy sneaking up behind me and act on instinct, then just rationalize it by making it Michael's instruction? Recently I've done everything I can to ignore them. Even in New York I tried to disregard them throughout that whole debacle, tried to be just my living self. But they're still here. I'm not in any danger, I feel okay, but here they are.

"Don't talk about that fucker," Sly says. "He is bad news."

"Papa Night knew we were here," Michael says.

They all look uncomfortable. Honestly, I'm enjoying this. I can't help but agree with Michael. "He did. You shitheels should think about that."

They all turn to me. "Why?" Alvin Crake asks, his bullet hole leaking blood along his nose. "What do we care?"

"You're his friend," Officer Graney says, flapping a hand at Michael. "You don't think straight around him."

Michael's eyebrows rise and he turns his head to display the ruined mess where my bullet exited. "We were friends, but this changed things."

"Fuck you!" I say. "What would you have done? You crossed Vern, you were going to die one way or another. Either I did it and lived, or I refused and died as well. You were already dead, man. I was saving my own life. You shouldn't have double-crossed Vern."

Michael sighs and nods. "That is true. But let's at least say I'm conflicted about how I feel."

I've done my best not to think too hard about New York or anything else in the time we've been in Vegas. In my experience, dwelling on the past is usually fraught with side effects. But I need to readdress that for a minute. I head into the bathroom, find some hydrogen peroxide to clean out these split knuckles, hissing at the sharp sting of it. Of course, that's nothing to what Burst Lip Asshole will be feeling right now. My hand is swollen and bruised too, but flexing my fingers it feels like nothing is broken this time. Lucky.

Something lingers with you, hmmm? Perhaps I can help?

That's what Papa Night said to me right before we left. I wanted nothing to do with him and still don't, but help how? He knew my haunts were here. If these fuckers really are ghosts, could I exorcise them? I've done my damnedest to ignore a lot of weird shit, but if I'm honest, there's been a fair amount of less than natural stuff happening around me lately. Is it such a leap to think maybe I could find the right kind of person to get rid of these hateful fuckers? I mean, a sane person would suggest a good psychiatrist, though no brain doctor is getting the dirty on my life. That would be problematic to say the least. But maybe it's not a brain issue.

I head back into the front room, sticking a couple of Band-Aids over the worst of my torn-up knuckles, and realize they're all staring at me. They do usually know my thoughts, after all. "Scared, motherfuckers?" I ask.

Michael nods slowly, then turns his head to look meaningfully at each of the others. "What then?" he asks. "Where do you think we'd go?"

They're all really uncomfortable now. Where *would* they go? They were all nasty people in their lives, even the damn cop. Cops are usually the worst of all in my experience.

I let them stew on it while I put the money in the safe, keeping a few hundred aside for pocket cash. I've arranged to meet Bridget outside the Bellagio at 11:00 p.m., which is only just over an hour away. An hour to have a couple of beers somewhere. I feel like being among people. Living people.

"I'll leave you fuckwits to your committee meeting," I say as I leave. "Enjoy your existential crisis."

TWO

WHILE VEGAS HAS BEEN EXCELLENT for income, I have to admit that I kinda hate the place. It's a living monument to greed and the worst of humanity. Shoulder to shoulder are people with more money than they could possibly spend and people who've just gambled away their last buck, their house, their future. And the glitz and lights and noise and cars. It's like excess is a god and he's vomited here in the desert. The place appalls me. Maybe that's part of the reason I have itchy feet. I need to talk to Bridget about leaving.

Leaving America for Monaco, or anywhere else really, is appealing right now for so many reasons. This country is going down the shithole fast. I don't know if anywhere else will be better, but I'd like to find out. Given how I feel about this town, I've found a few places here and there that are kinder on the eye and the ear. One is The Dali Room. It's only a few minutes' walk from our apartment, and ten minutes or so in a cab to go and meet Bridget later. It's a hole-in-the-wall place, with herringbone tiled floors and a wooden bar. It's dim inside and on a weeknight it's pretty calm.

I choose a stool at the bar and order a beer. I've only had one sip when Michael on the stool next to me says, "Heads up."

The rest of my ghosts are all loitering around behind the bar, but the bartender doesn't know that. He's idly staring at nothing. I glance sidelong at Michael, one eyebrow raised, and he nods back toward the door. Three men have entered. Two are gorillas, the kind of goon who's mostly muscle with a walnut for a brain. Lackeys. Mooks who follow orders. But the one in the middle is different. Small, wiry, with slicked-back black hair and a black goatee oiled to a point. His skin is a deep tan, but his eyes are piercing blue, standing out against his dark, neat suit. He slowly pans his gaze across the small bar like he's looking for someone, and as his eyes fall on me, I feel a deep stab of burning pain at my hip. A slight involuntary flinch makes me shift on the stool and the goatee asshole points one long finger at me.

What the hell hurt me? I'll have to think about that later, as those two gorillas are heading right over. I've beaten bigger and meaner dudes before, but two of them in this cramped space is a challenge. And two fights in one night after such a long spell of peace seems unfair. Then again, life is anything but fair.

I slide off the stool, keeping it between me and them. If they get too close, the first of them will be wearing it for a hat. But they stop about six feet away, standing far enough apart that I'd have trouble getting past them if I made a run for it, but not so far apart that I could easily slip between them. I'm not the kind of guy who runs anyway.

Goatee smiles, anything but friendly, and wanders up. "What's your name?"

I frown and shake my head. "Not in the mood for company tonight. Fuck off."

His smile widens. "A tough guy? I'm Jose Santiago. I think we need to talk."

"We really don't, buddy."

"Careful, Eli," Michael says. "There's something weird about this guy."

"Yeah, he feels a little like that Papa Night fucker," Graney says.

"Watch yourself," Sly says.

The fuck are they all so concerned about all of a sudden? They always used to whoop and holler whenever I was in danger, excited to see me hurt. I've made a hobby of disappointing them. There has been a fundamental shift in their attitude here and I'm not sure I like it much. But right now, Jose Santiago is a more pressing concern.

He leans forward. "Yes. We do. This can be easy or hard. You have something that doesn't belong to you and I want it back. Give it to me and this is all finished."

"I don't have anything of yours, asshole."

The gorillas bristle, itching for a fight. Santiago raises one hand to stay them a moment. "Not mine," he says. "But not yours. That's the point."

"The ring," Michael says.

What fucking ring? Then I remember the stab of burning pain at my hip. The heavy gold and onyx signet ring I took off Burst Lip Asshole and stuffed into my pocket. I forgot all about it.

Santiago's smile widens again. "I see your brain has caught up with our conversation." He holds out one hand, palm up. His fingers are long and slim and impeccably manicured. That alone pisses me off. "Let me have it and we need never see each other again."

Now fancy hands or not, I don't like this guy. Some people are the human equivalent of a bad smell. No matter where the smell is from, you just don't like it. Take those fucking lilies they always have at funerals. Symbolic of the soul of the departed or some shit. They have such a strong perfume, and they're flowers, supposed to be beautiful. But I fucking hate them. Whether it's because I associate the smell with death or something, I don't know. The fact is, they may be a beautiful and calming flower, but I hate how they look, how they smell. Hell, I hate that they exist. And now and then we come across people like that. I hate that Santiago exists. For whatever reason, it doesn't matter. So, there's no way I'm giving him anything he wants.

I'm also a curious person. It gets me in trouble, because someone who goes through life never asking questions is usually happier. You ever notice how the happiest people are the most fucking stupid? If a person is smart enough to ask questions, they rarely get good enough answers, and that leads to discontent. It takes a real idiot to be happy all the time. Regardless, I have questions. Who the fuck is this smell of a person? How did he find me? How does he know I have the ring? Why did the thing burn me? *How* did it burn me? Why is he so desperate to get it back? Because he may be trying to act calm, but I can see the concern in his eyes.

See, that's a lot of questions. And the search for answers will only bring me unhappiness. But what can I say? I'm a man at the mercy of his nature.

"Eli!" Michael says in alarm, at the exact same moment as both Officer Graney and Sly Barclay say, "Oh shit."

But already the barstool is in my hand sweeping upwards. One leg of it cracks Santiago right in his oily beard and he yelps and staggers backwards. Then I have two hands gripping the seat and I stab the feet of it at the gorilla on the left. His hands are coming up, but too slow. Two out of four blunt points of wood drive hard into him. One in the eye, one in the throat. He makes an interesting noise as blood floods over his cheek, but I don't have time to enjoy it. Santiago is down on his side, groaning, but the other gorilla has had time to get moving.

I sweep the barstool hard to my right, but he has both hands up and the wood smashes to pieces across his meaty forearms.

"Hey, what the fuck?" the bartender yells, but I don't have time to converse.

Using the moment I bought with the barstool, I skip to my right, trying to get alongside the big fucker. Now the thing about big people is they carry a lot of weight, but their knees are just the same as yours and mine. Sure, if they're smart enough to not skip leg day their muscles are strong, but all joints have weak points. A big, heavy dude's knees especially. As the gorilla draws back a fist to clobber me, I lift my foot and stamp down hard on the side of his knee with my heel. There's a snap like a gunshot, probably his ACL or meniscus separating, or both, and he squeals like a pig as his leg folds up underneath him.

To his credit he still delivers the punch, but he's already dropping and I turn to catch it on the shoulder. His fist is like rock and my left arm goes instantly numb and weak. Thankfully, I have another one. Pivoting on the ball of my foot I bring a sweeping punch around right into his cheekbone. The impact is satisfyingly solid, but the repeat pain through my already bruised and torn-up knuckles less so. Not to worry, he grunts and goes floppy, tries to put his hands down, but manages to miss the floor and face-plants.

I'm already running, the bartender still yelling behind me, several people screaming or shouting encouragement. It's funny how different people respond to violence. The night is cool and fresh and I run to the corner and turn down the next street. Fortune smiles and there's a cab cruising toward me, light on. A wave and he stops. I jump in.

"Bellagio, thanks."

"You got it." The driver has a huge smile in a dark face. "Having a good night?" he asks.

As we drive back past the Dali Room, I see Santiago leaning on the door of the bar, one hand pressed to his chin, looking furious. "Actually, yeah," I tell the driver. "I'm having the best night in a long while."

"You're gonna regret that soon, I reckon," Alvin Crake says, twisting around from the front seat.

I flip him the bird and settle back, trying to ignore Michael, Sly, Dwight, and Graney all crowded into the back with me.

THREE

I NEED TIME AND SPACE TO THINK about everything that's happened tonight, but first I have to put this ring somewhere safe. Literally a safe is probably my best option, but that Santiago fucker managed to track me down somehow, so the one in our apartment is maybe not a good idea. How did he find me? Was it something mundane like CCTV? Seems unlikely. It feels like he was able to find the ring itself. And the way it burned me when he arrived... Not good. I have somewhere else nearby in mind.

I ask the cab driver to stop on Las Vegas Boulevard a little before the Bellagio. I tip him an extra five bucks and wish him a good night. As I get out of the cab, Sly says, "Silver."

Making sure no one is close enough to hear me talking to myself, I say, "What?"

"Put it in silver, man. He won't be able to trace it that way."

"How do you know that?"

Sly shrugs, lighting a fresh joint. Blood drips from his gaping chest wound but never reaches the sidewalk. "Just do. Seems I know a few things now I wasn't privy to in the land of the living."

"He's right," Michael says. "Silver should work."

"Gift shop over there." Graney points. "Find something there, maybe."

"Why are you assholes so helpful all of a sudden?"

"Yeah, what the fuck?" Dwight says, looking with a confused expression at his cohorts. "Fuck cocheese here, I wanna see him kilt!"

Michael shakes his head. "Trust you to be too stupid to get it."

"Hey, fuck you too!"

Michael ignores him, turns back to me. "Seriously, for now just make sure that Santiago weirdo can't follow you anymore. If you put that thing inside silver, it'll block him. Like lead with Superman's X-ray vision, yeah? There's a reason for all those legends about silver bullets and werewolves and vampires and shit. Silver disrupts certain energies. Trust us, okay?"

I find a small solid silver pill box in the gift shop. Not cheap, but I feel like there's little choice right now. Outside, I drop the ring inside and take a photo of it with my phone before I close the lid. I think I'm going to need to study the weird symbol carved into the black stone. My gaggle of ghosts are all visibly relieved the moment it's sealed away. Except Dwight. He still has no idea what's going on. I guess that's been a lifelong condition for him.

Then I call Stanley. He runs a little boutique café not far from Planet Hollywood and lives right there in the back. He can't afford another rent, understandably. We became friendly a couple of months ago when we got drunk together at Beer Park. I was waiting for Bridget, he was lamenting the wife who ran out on him with a dealer from Circus Circus Casino. "She ran away to the fucking circus, can you believe the irony?" he said to me through a haze of good single malt scotch. I know a little something about losing the love of your life, and I was feeling friendly, so I hung with him.

Stanley is a good guy, strangely out of place in the glitz of Vegas. Somewhere in his mid-forties, but he looks over fifty already. Plenty of hair, but all of it white, he's short, friendly, going a little soft around the middle. We've become buddies of a kind, and I eat at his place a lot now, we go out drinking sometimes. I think he'll do me a favor.

"You jonesing for a drink?" he says by way of answering the phone.

"Why, are you?"

He laughs. "Not gonna lie, I'm way ahead of you." His voice is a little slurred. "But I'm drinking at home and about ready to drop. Another time?"

"Actually, I just wanted to ask a favor. You got a good safe in your place?"

"Of course, why?"

"Can I leave something with you for a while?"

When he lets me in his eyes are red and wet, his shoulders hanging low like a suit jacket on a too-small clothes hanger. Sadness washes off him in waves. "This gonna get me in trouble?"

I smile. "Nah, it's nothing illegal. Just a secret from Bridget, so I can't keep it in our safe." The lie comes easily to me and I hope I'm right. If these haunts are right about the silver, Stan has nothing to worry about.

We go through the café, stools upended on tables, a smell of pine-fresh bleach in the air, and there's a small office before the main rooms he uses as an apartment. The safe is under the desk and he opens it up, I tuck the silver case.

"Pretty," Stan says. "Some kinda anniversary?"

"Not really. Just a surprise."

"I remember when I used to do shit like that for Keri. Just random acts of love and kindness, you know? I wonder why I bothered." He glances up at me, sways slightly. "Sorry, man. I hope it's different for you. But you never know, you know? Shit changes in an instant. I was happy until she said she was leaving me. Apparently she'd been unhappy for a long time. How did I not know?"

I see he's reached the melancholy stage of drunkenness. "Some things just aren't meant to work out, I guess." It's a lame thing to say, but what else is there? Suggest he wasn't good enough for her? I don't know their story.

"Have a drink with me, eh?" He heads through into his apartment.

He's doing me a favor, so I don't feel like I can just walk out, even though I want to. I follow him, sit on a sofa while he slumps in a well-worn armchair. Some game show is playing on the TV, the sound muted. He pours me a bourbon, pours himself another twice the size.

"To women, while we have the pleasure of their company," he says, raising his glass.

"I'll drink to that."

I stay for as long as I feel is polite, but only have the one drink. He's nodding in the armchair anyway, eyes hooded, and I excuse myself. I wish I could make his life better somehow, but maybe he just has to grieve for a while. I understand that.

I stroll back down the Boulevard toward the Bellagio. I feel lighter, and realize I've had the sensation of someone watching me all night and now it's gone.

The fingers of my left arm are tingling, my shoulder still throbbing where that gorilla's punch landed, and my right hand aches like a son of a bitch. My knuckles have bled through the Band-Aids a little, but otherwise I'm in pretty good shape for someone who's had two street fights in one night. And honestly, I'm a little elated by it all. Plus, I feel like I have something to do. It's been great to hang out with Bridget, enjoy her ability to rake in the cash, plan for a future of beaches and high living. But I've been so damn passive throughout, I didn't realize how much I was missing a purpose. Being the boyfriend and bodyguard is good, but not entirely fulfilling on a personal level. Now I have my own focus, and I also feel like I shouldn't bring Bridget into it too much.

"Hiding things from the wife is the first sign of the end," Graney says with a wolfish cackle.

"Yeah, man," Alvin says. "You'll kill her passion in an instant if you start lying."

I ignore them. Like Alvin fucking Crake is any kind of relationship counselor. I need a long conversation with these assholes. Figure out this attitude change in them. Seems that existential crisis they had was more powerful than I thought. I also need to find someone like Papa Night, as I have some ideas circling, like sharks in dark water, ready to surge up and start taking bites. I don't think about it too hard, because I don't want the peanut gallery to think too hard on it either.

Bridget slings her arms around my neck and pulls herself up for a long kiss the moment she sees me. This woman fires me up inside, she's so beautiful and confident and downright amazing.

"Good night?" I ask.

She grins and hefts her bag. "Remember what you banked for me earlier? Twice as much again here. It's been a *very* good night. Let's take this home and celebrate."

I get butterflies immediately and ignore the groans and slurs from my ghosts. They hate it when I get laid, knowing they'll never enjoy anything like it again. They all make themselves scarce when it happens too, thankfully. I'd half-expect them to hang around and be the worst kind of voyeurs, but maybe it's too much for them.

"What happened here?" Bridget picks up my hand, looking at the Band-Aids.

I don't want to lie to her, but I do plan to omit a lot of what went down tonight. Once I have a better idea of what's happening, I'll tell her all about it. I ignore the scoffing ghosts around us and say, "Couple of idiots saw me leave with the cash earlier and jumped me."

"Eli!" Her face is shocked.

"Hey, it's fine, really. We had a dust-up, but they came off worse and the money is safe at home." I realize I still hadn't started carrying a gun again yet, and maybe I should.

She nods, but she's not happy. "I'm glad to hear that. But you need to be more careful. It's not like you to be seen. Followed."

A feel a flush of shame at that. She's right. I've been getting complacent these last few weeks. "It was a wake-up call, yeah. I'll pay more attention. But it's all good, I promise. Nothing to spoil our night."

She smiles crookedly. "Well let's get home and I'll kiss it better. Anywhere else get hurt?"

"I can think of a couple of places that might need kissing, yeah."

FOUR

BRIDGET SLEEPS DEEPLY AFTER SEX, every time. I don't want to blow my own trumpet too much, but I feel like she gets exactly what she needs from me, and I'm happy with that. But I can't sleep. Even after all this time out of the life, I'm often on edge at night.

I'm sitting in the gloom of our living room, nothing but the dim glow of streetlights outside and the light of my phone as I look at the photo I took of the ring. The heavy gold weight of it is one thing, but that stone gets to me. When I got undressed earlier... Well, when Bridget undressed me, I saw a red mark on my hip where it had sat in my pocket when Santiago walked in. Thankfully Bridget didn't seem to notice, her eyes were elsewhere, so I didn't have to field any more questions, but it wasn't just a random sensation. The ring actually burned me. It's still tender to the touch.

"Santiago activated it." Sly is sitting opposite me on the couch, his internal organs glittering in the low light. I realize Graney is next to him, Michael leaning against the kitchen doorframe, Alvin in the other armchair, and Dwight is standing with his back to me, staring out the window, the lights of suburban Las Vegas a dim orange glow.

"Activated?"

Sly nods. "Bad shit, man. Leave it alone."

"You should listen," Graney says. "We told you Papa Night was bad news and look what happened there."

I flex my aching hand, stiffening up from the bruising, and stare at the symbol in the photo. The black stone is engraved with a kind of spiral, bisected by two converging lines. It's fine and beautiful work, at the same time intriguing and disquieting.

"You lot were crowing about the trouble I was in there. You're always disappointed when I survive. What's changed?"

They clam up, if anything they look a little contrite. I remember what Michael said earlier. *What then? Where do you think we'd go?*

"You really are all having some kind of existential crisis, huh?"

"Just leave this ring shit alone," Alvin Crake says. "Get on with your life. You got it good now, fuck ya."

"And you all hate that. But suddenly you don't want me dead anymore."

"I'd love to see you die, cocheese. It would be worth it, you ask me."

"Only because you're too stupid to consider the consequences," Sly says.

"Fuck you!" Dwight spits a bunch a racist expletives and dives over the couch, wrestling Sly to the ground. They trade punches, Sly's joint bursting in a cloud of sparks and smoke under Dwight's knuckles.

I ignore them, turn to Michael. "What did he mean, when he said Santiago activated the ring?"

"We feel energies where we are," Michael says. "Hard to explain, but it's like ripples in water, or wind pushing away smoke. There's shift and movement around us all the time, and when someone living manipulates something…supernatural, I guess, we see the eddies and ripples. We saw it when Santiago walked in and then the ring burned you. Seems some people have genuine supernatural powers."

"Like Papa Night?"

"Yeah."

This is too much to think about, but I have to follow it through. "You said 'where we are'. Where are you?"

"No idea."

"And that's what's got you scared?"

"I guess."

"I don't think scared is the right word," Graney says. "It has us confused."

"I'm fucking scared," Sly says. His eye is swollen shut and his lip is bleeding, but Dwight is nowhere to be seen. Sly grins. "I kick his ass every time, but he will not learn."

"You're not always around me," I say. "Where do you go then?"

They shrug, look around at each other.

"I guess it's kinda like being asleep," Michael says. "You're like this beacon in a foggy night, so we find you easy. The rest of the time we're in the fog, but I never really notice. Time is… Well, there isn't really time here."

"For nearly two years I was hiding out in Canada, things were pretty quiet, I hardly saw you. Now and then you'd crop up and go away again."

"Two years?" Michael shakes his head. "Might as well have been last week."

I think about it for a while. *What then? Where do you think we'd go?*

"So now you've been spooked by Papa Night, and the things that happened then, and you're thinking maybe if something happens to me, you won't be lingering around in the fog anymore. You'll end up somewhere else."

"Maybe."

"And you think it won't be such a nice place?" I can't help but grin.

"Fuck you, man," Graney says. "You think you'll go anywhere better?"

"I don't know. But I'm not dead yet. I'm trying to atone for my sins. Besides, I don't even know if I believe any of that Heaven and Hell shit. Maybe your brain just switches off and that's it. No one has any memory of before they were born, so why would it be any different after you're dead?"

"You just end and that's it?" Alvin asks. "Fuck, what's the damn point in that?"

I frown at him. "Why does there have to be a point?"

"Regardless," Michael says. "We've decided that maybe you should enjoy life a while and we'll all just get along."

"Fuck getting along," Alvin says.

"Yeah," Graney agrees. "I don't know about getting along. But just don't die yet. I hate you, but you should probably stay alive for now. While we think about this some more."

I can't help laughing. "I have never met a more conflicted bunch of idiots. You think you'll be able to do something about your situation? Plan a new ghostly future?"

"Screw you, man," Sly says.

"Help me then. Help me figure this out." I hold up my phone, the photo of the signet ring.

"Fuck you," Alvin says.

"Yeah," Graney agrees.

Michael shrugs, Sly lights another joint. Where the hell does he get them? Dwight is back, battered and bleeding, subdued in the corner. Graney scowls.

"What a waste of time you all are," I say. I'm starting to feel tired after all.

As I get up to head for the bathroom, Bridget appears at the bedroom door. "You talking to someone?" She's blurry with sleep.

I wave my phone, then drop it in my pocket. "Just Stanley. Drunk and melancholy again."

"Huh." She nods, eyes still mostly closed, and goes back to bed.

FIVE

"**T**HIS IS BULLSHIT, MAN!**" Alvin's face bears the same combination of disdain and fear as the rest of them.

"Yeah, don't mess with this stuff, man." Sly isn't smoking a joint, so he's really distracted as he stands half-visible in the bright morning sun.

I glance at Michael and he shrugs, his face resigned. Can ghosts get depressed? Just my luck to be haunted by ghosts with mental health issues. Then again, I still think maybe these assholes are *my* mental health issues. And in this day and age, it's hard to imagine anyone without some form of brain trauma.

Madame Yennifer, she sounds like a try-hard. FORTUNES READ, LOST LOVED ONES CONTACTED the sign says. Her small shop is all diaphanous drapery and soft music, and the cloying stink of incense burning as I walk in. A few shelves of trinkets—crystal balls, dream catchers, angel figurines. It's awful. Reminds me of the front of Papa Night's place, but that *was* a front, to hide stuff far more sinister. This? I think it's all front.

"You are troubled."

Ugh. Her voice is like wind chimes. She moves like she's made of smoke. Kinda hot though, I expected an old woman, but she's barely thirty. She lifts aside the curtain she appeared through.

"Shall we?"

"You should just fuck this phony, cocheese. That's the only way you'll get anything out of her."

Graney chuckles as he walks beside me. "You're a dipshit, Carver. How did you not end up in jail before you were out of your teens?"

They're all suddenly relaxed and jovial again. "No ripples in the fog?" I ask Michael.

He's already in her chamber, the other side of a round table with a black velvet cloth over it. He shakes his head. "There's nothing for you here."

"Sorry, what did you say?" Yennifer's brow is creased.

"Just talking to myself."

She sits and gestures for me to sit opposite. When I take a seat, she places her hands on the table, fingers interlaced, and smiles softly. "What do you need?"

"A genuine medium would be a start."

The crease between her eyebrows flickers ever so briefly, but the smile stays. "I can help, if you'll allow it." She slips her palms over a crystal ball on a stand in the center of the table. "A reading, perhaps? Know your future? Or your past."

"She can tell the past!" Graney says with a bark of laughter. "Man, she *is* good."

The others laugh, even Michael.

"You see the dead around me?" I ask.

The smile slips away. "You suffer from grief?" she asks.

"Nah, I suffer from fucking ghosts. They tail me like tattered flags in my wake. You tell me if you see them and I'll know if you're genuine or not."

She sits back, lips pursed, eyes narrowed. Then she takes a deep breath and slips into an act. Her eyes close, she nods slightly, turns her face a little left, a little right. "I see a…a woman. And a child."

My heart stutters just slightly.

"Lucky guess,' Alvin says. "Ask her to describe them."

"The woman is elderly, but kind."

"There you go, she's blown it already," Sly says. "She's a fake, man."

"Tell her to blow you, cocheese!"

"Michael, come here, please," I say.

Yennifer pops her eyes open, looks around. Michael is wearing a crooked smile, he's enjoying himself for once. He stands at my shoulder. I gesture up at him. "Describe this dead fucker right here."

Yennifer looks from me to the empty space beside me and back again. "I don't… I'm not sure we can really work together, Mr. Carver. Perhaps you should go."

Michael glances at me and there's something serious as hell in his eyes. He leans forward, puts his fingers against the crystal ball, and for a moment his concentration is intense, his face twisted like he's in pain. The other ghosts start yelling at him to stop, then Michael yelps as if he's been burned and the ball tips off the stand with a *thunk* and rolls into Yennifer's lap.

"You fucking idiot!" Alvin shouts.

Yennifer screams and leaps up, the ball dropping heavily to the floor as she backs away from it like it's alive. The other ghosts are furious. Except Michael. He's smiling a little, but looking at me with one eyebrow raised.

"His doubt was all we had!" Graney yells, blood spraying from his ruined throat. The low light glints off his police badge.

"You're really real," I say, almost a whisper. My heart is racing.

"Who do you think saved you at Vern's place with that wheelbarrow?"

"I thought maybe a cat, a bit of luck…"

"You denied it then, you denied it so hard throughout the whole thing in New York. No more."

"You are fucking crazy, man," Sly says, fading out.

"But if you lot won't help me, what difference does it make?" I ask Michael.

"Who are you talking to?" Yennifer wails, her voice high and panicked. She's looking all around the small room like she's about to be attacked. "Get out! Get out get out get out!"

The ghosts all vanish, their angry voices fading, so I turn to leave. Then turn back. Her hands come up like she needs to defend herself.

"Chill out, okay? I'm not going to hurt you, and I will leave. I just want to ask you one thing." My head is spinning, too much in flux right now, but I have this one thing to focus on. I pull up the photo of the ring on my phone, zoom in to the stone and the carved symbol. "This mean anything to you? You ever seen it before?"

She's trembling all over as she leans in for a look. "No. No idea. Now, please leave."

When I step out into the bright day, there's a guy on a bench across the sidewalk staring at me. He looks homeless, raggedy layers of clothing, gray stubble on his chin, wisps of gray hair curling out from under a wool cap full of holes. He raises a bottle in a brown paper bag in a kind of toast, smiles at me. What few teeth he has are yellow.

I return the smile, nod. No harm in being friendly, it might not be his fault he fell on hard times. Everyone has a story and some of them are tragic. Talking of tragic, my ghosts are nowhere to be seen.

The homeless guy tips his head to one side, eyes narrowed. "She didn't fool you, huh." His voice is gravelly, thick with drink, probably smokes, though he isn't smoking now.

I jab a thumb back over my shoulder. "Madame Yennifer? She's a crook."

"I like to sit here and watch people come outta there. Some are cryin', you know, bawlin' their eyes out like they just met their dead gramma or something. Some look scared. I allas wunnered if she had the goods."

"Nah. She's got nothing."

"How do you know that? Yanno, for sure?"

"Inside information."

He cackles a wheezy laugh. "Have a good day, yeah?"

"Yeah, man. You too." I start to turn away, then stop. "You need a few bucks? Something to eat?"

"Fuck yeah."

I dig in my pocket and find a twenty, hand it over.

He takes it with a strangely gentle touch, then smiles softly. "Thank ya. Really."

"You're welcome."

As I start to walk away, he calls out. "There's another, across town."

"Another what?"

He waves a grubby hand at Madame Yennifer's place. "Another one a'these folks. Luxana, she goes by." He tells me an address I never heard of.

"How far is that?"

"Dozen blocks maybe."

"You think this Luxana is the real deal?"

He laughs. "You know that shit, man, not me. But I sometimes sit outside her place too."

"Thanks. I'll check her out." I wish my heart would settle. Feels like my world has tilted a little off-axis. They're real. They're really real.

He nods, gestures with the twenty by way of thanks, then sits back to drink from his bottle.

SIX

s I'm heading down the street, I get a text from Bridget.

Lunch?

It's early for that, so I guess she's had a good morning at the tables. I text back, *Across town right now, running an errand. Rain check?*

What errand? What are you up to?

Secret biz. You okay to skip lunch?

Maybe I'll find a high roller, take him out.

As long as you fleece him and don't fuck him.

She texts back a smiley face and I send a love heart. It's all so easy with Bridget, no pretense, no jealousy or suspicion. I feel bad for not telling her more about what's happening, but I'm honestly not sure how much she would take. The last thing I want to do is scare her away.

As I stride the blocks toward this Luxana's place, I make a decision. When I see her later, I'll show her the photo of the ring and explain all that happened there. See how much she believes. And then I'm coming clean too about the errand I'm on, because really, that's what I want. More info about this symbol, this group, the weird sensation I got from the ring in my pocket when that asshole found me. *How* that asshole found me. I know I'm doing all I can to not think too hard on the peanut gallery and what Michael did back there.

"Black limo on your left, don't look."

Talk of the dead, there he is, walking beside me.

"What about it?" I ask.

Michael sniffs, I see sunlight glint off the blood as it drops from his ruined head. "Been tailing you for about two blocks now."

"Where's the rest of the gang?"

Michael shrugs. "Around. They're mad at me."

"I saw that. Why did you do it?"

"No more pussyfooting around."

"That's not all though, right? You guys are scared."

"Maybe. Look out."

People like me, we exist like cats. It's ingrained. They say a cat never enters a room until it knows all the exits and dead ends. That's why they always pause in doorways. Fuck knows if that's true, but it tracks. You stay alive in a world like mine by thinking the same way. And these guys know it. The limo slides to a quick halt at the curb right in front of me and I know already I'm mid-block. There was a side street about fifty paces back, an alley another fifty paces ahead, and the next side street beyond that. Right now there's nothing but the road on my left and a solid wall with windows on my right. The doorway into the building is on the other side of the goons who pile out of the car.

"Three behind," Michael says. "Didn't see that car following too, but must have been."

I don't need to look to picture the second car, pulled up to the curb between me and that first side street. Well played, assholes. Classic pincer. How did they find me again?

Worry about that later. Three behind, and three from the limo. That's six. I can see the silhouette of the limo driver, sitting there ready. "The driver of the other car still in his seat?" I ask.

"No," Michael says. "That idiot is one of the three now on the sidewalk in a line."

He knows the score too, I can hear the amusement in his voice. He sees there's an out here and he knows I'm going to go for it. Just got to pick my moment. A moment of overconfidence by that driver behind me will hopefully be their undoing.

"You are a slippery customer," one of the three in front of me says and I realize it's Jose Santiago. His voice is a little clipped, talking without moving his mouth much. The goatee has been shaved off and there's a line of stitches under his chin. I did a good job with that barstool.

"Take it easy," Graney says. "I get the feeling these guys won't hesitate to murder in broad daylight."

"Thanks for your concern, cop."

He bristles, but clamps his lips. The traffic on the street is medium, but constant. A few people are walking the sidewalks, but no one within a hundred paces of us right at this moment. A young couple are on their way, though, and a lone guy talking into a cell phone right behind them.

"Group of women with shopping bags just crossing the side street behind us," Graney says.

I nod. That gives these guys maybe a minute tops before things are complicated by the arrival of Joe Public.

I gesture at my chin. "Suits you."

Santiago scowls. "Just give it to me!"

"How did you find me this time?" I'm genuinely interested, because the ring is nowhere near me. It also buys me time. They want it badly enough they won't just drop me in the street.

"I have many and varied skills, Mr. Carver."

"You found out my name too. Does that mean you have some idea of my body count? Might want to rethink hassling me." Sometimes bravado pays off, sometimes it doesn't. I can see Santiago doesn't care, but the two goons either side of him are nervous, I see it in their eyes. I'm guessing they heard about the two gorillas in the bar last night, and maybe learned some of my history from Santiago.

"Shoppers about forty feet behind the goons," Graney says.

The couple and cell phone guy are about the same distance behind Santiago.

"We know all about you and we are not scared of you, Mr. Carver. Let's make this simple. All previous transgressions forgiven if you simply give me the ring. We need never see each other again."

I don't believe that for a moment. He'll come for revenge, but the ring is clearly the first priority. And it's my leverage. His eyes flick past my shoulder then back to me. He's clocked the shoppers coming, he'll move any second.

"Just take him!" Santiago snaps, wincing as he inadvertently moves his jaw too much.

My hand is still aching from previous trauma, but I'm going to have to suck that up. Both Santiago and the three behind me think I haven't seen them, so it's time to drop a few surprises. I hope my swollen and aching hand doesn't affect my aim too much.

Moments like this, lots of stuff happens at once. Prioritizing is the key to survival. I drop and roll backwards, pulling the CZ 75 9mm from my waistband as I go. I'm not above murder in broad daylight either. I've already made sure no cameras are looking this way. As sure I can be anyway. I want to pop a bullet in Santiago, but he's less of a threat now, so I squeeze off one round to the heavy on his right and catch him center-chest. He drops. The other heavy is drawing as Santiago dives straight for the limo. I twist and come up running the other way, my back itching because I know that one heavy is drawing a bead on me, but there's three here. Sure enough, they all have guns in some stage of readiness. I fire three times, hoping to drop them all, but even my great shooting skills aren't up to that, not moving like I am. But I get the first right between the eyes, the second in the shoulder of his gun arm, and miss the third.

No time to worry, I drop again, straight into a forward roll this time. The screaming has started from the people on the street, some car tires screeching as people swerve or brake in a panic at the gunfire. The one heavy behind me squeezes off rapid shots, trying to track me, but I keep moving. My nerves are on fire, waiting for that punch of pain to let me know he got a hit but it doesn't come. The one left standing in front of me now is wide-eyed and open-mouthed as I come to my feet less than a foot from him and slam my gun butt up under his chin. The idiot should have abandoned shooting for brawling and he might have had me at such close quarters. More fool him.

He staggers back, dazed, and I duck around the one I shot in the shoulder. To his credit, he's grabbing for me, still trying to do his job, but that's his last mistake. I grab him instead and swing him around just as the heavy who'd been beside Santiago fires again. Except now I have a human shield. He bucks and jerks as his compatriot's bullets slam into his back and arm, then I'm dropping him and diving in through the open front passenger door of the car they arrived in. Here's my gamble. If the keys aren't in it, I'm in trouble.

I scramble across the passenger seat, cramming my long legs and large frame into the driver's seat and allow myself a smile to see not only are the keys in it, but they left it running. I slam it into gear and roar away from the curb, wincing at the screeching tires of cars trying to stop behind me.

"Damn, son," Graney says from the passenger seat. "Impressive."

Michael, Sly, Dwight and Alvin are lined up in the back seat whooping and hollering. The rear window shatters as one of the heavies gets a final shot away, and my ghosts only cheer louder.

"Acrobatic motherfucker!" Sly says, with something approaching respect.

These ghosts have truly changed their tune.

Michael nods once, gives me a soft smile.

"Once you're safely away, you might wanna look at that though," Graney says, pointing at my upper right arm.

It's soaked with blood and, as I notice it, the searing burn makes it to my brain. One of those fuckers shot me after all.

SEVEN

AFTER DRIVING A FEW BLOCKS and making sure the limo wasn't tailing me, I pull over to tend to the wound. It's superficial, thankfully. Burns like a son of a bitch, and bleeds a lot, but it's not too serious. It'll scab over in twenty-four hours. Someone left their jacket on the back seat, so I rip the cotton lining out of it and use that to strap up a bandage around my arm. It'll be sore for a while, but nothing to worry about as long as I keep it clean. I've suffered way worse and survived.

Now the adrenaline is settling down I feel a little nauseated, but that's normal. I'm also feeling a moment of regret. I should have shot Santiago after all. I was right in the fact that he wasn't a threat at that moment, being the only one unarmed. The way he dived for cover like the chickenshit he is was proof enough of that. But he is perhaps a bigger threat in the long run. How did he find me this time?

"Some kinda seer," Sly says from the back seat, wreathed again in joint smoke.

"Seer?"

Sly nods, passes the joint to Alvin and sits forward. "My grandma used to tell the tales, some people can scry. I don't really get it all, but perhaps he can go into a kind of a trance and travel astrally, look around for you. He met you once, so he knows your aura. Like a dog with a scent, he can look for you that way. Once he gets close, they search the old-fashioned way."

It's the longest speech Sly has made in as long as I can remember, and it makes some kind of sense. And it only confirms my thought that I should have shot him just now when I had the chance. Still, no point in dwelling on the past. I was making decisions then to stay alive and it worked.

"So that means he can track me again any time?"

Sly shrugs, sits back.

"You have to assume so," Michael says. "But a big city this populated? Can't be too easy."

"Might have bought myself some time then."

"Maybe give up finding this Luxana bitch and deal with the problem at hand," Alvin says, passing the joint on to Graney.

The cop nods, takes a draw. Smoke curls out of his blood-soaked throat. "Yeah, he's right. Focus."

"Focus, cocheese." Dwight is strangely subdued, the usual manic demeanor suppressed.

These fuckers are truly uncomfortable. I have them on the ropes in a way and I'm reluctant to give that up. Besides, I need information. "I'm not a seer," I say. "I need to know who these bastards are and this Luxana might be my only lead. If that bothers you, maybe just fuck off. The real problem at hand is these assholes trying to kill me. And before you say, 'Just give the ring back' you know we're past that point now."

I pull the makeshift bandage tight around my arm and use the jacket to wipe down everything in the car that I touched. Then I climb out and walk away quickly along the sidewalk. I need to replace my shirt, the shoulder and arm of it are bright red with drying blood. And I need to not be so noticeable. The jacket comes in handy, so I keep it, slung casually over my shoulder to mask the injury. But it's out of place, a smart suit jacket with my jeans and T-shirt. A thrift store up ahead provides an option. It only takes a moment to find a short-sleeved button-up shirt that fits, plain black cotton, the sleeves long enough to cover my makeshift bandage. My arm throbs underneath it, but I do my best to ignore that. My bloodstained T-shirt and the mook's jacket get crammed in a garbage can on the sidewalk not far from the shop and I'm back in business. A little more urgent now though, seeing as Santiago can find me regardless.

The drive made up a couple of extra blocks so it only takes me a few more minutes to walk to the address for Luxana the homeless guy gave me. It's a plain-looking apartment block in a residential area. As I frown up at the building, wondering if I've been led up the garden path by a drunk, the man himself strolls up to stand next to me.

"Took ya long enough."

"The fuck is this?" Dwight asks.

"More than he looks," Graney says.

No shit, collective Sherlocks. I guess I'm starting to get used to this weird stuff, because I'm not really surprised. "Had a little distraction on the way here," I tell him.

"No time for side quests, friend." He grins and gestures with the bottle. "Apartment 419, fourth floor. Tell her Elvis sent you."

"Elvis?"

"Uh huh huh." He grins and walks away.

I choose not to pursue that any further and head into the building. The doors are locked, with all the apartments and their call buttons on a panel outside. There's no name next to 419. I press the button and wait. A small lens, like a shark's eye, stares at me from above the buttons and I wonder if Luxana is using it. I'm reaching up to press the button again when a voice says, "Yes?"

"Is that Luxana?"

"Who's this?"

"My name is Eli. I need your help. Elvis sent me."

"Did he now?"

Even through the tinny speaker, her voice is low and soft, sultry in a way. I feel like she's not putting it on, like she really talks that way. Which is actually kind of weird. "Said you were the real deal."

"He's very kind. Well, I know I'm going to regret this, but come on up."

The door buzzes and clicks and I push it open, head to the elevators and press number four. When I come out of the elevator, a door halfway along the hallway is standing open, a middle-aged woman framed by it. She's quite striking to look at, sharp features, but not harsh, long brown hair held back in a loose ponytail, floral cotton dress and bare feet. She nods when she sees me and it looks almost like recognition.

"Come on in. Bring your friends with you."

I glance around and see the five fuckwits all gathered in the hallway nearby, all looking a little pensive. "This is better already, eh?"

Michael allows a half-smile, but Dwight, Alvin, Graney and Sly all grimace.

"Probably don't do this, man" Alvin says.

"Why not?"

"I don't trust her."

"Me either, cocheese. Unless you plan to simply rape her and run, there's nothing for you here."

"What the fuck is your fascination with rape, you disgusting fucking racist?" I ask him. "Seriously, you have a real problem."

"No one would ever fuck him, so it was the only action he ever got," Alvin says.

Even Graney and Sly looked appalled at that.

"Maybe no one wanted anything to do with him because he's such a fucking awful piece of shit," I suggest, and don't wait for an answer.

Inside, Luxana's apartment is small but homey. The door leads to a short hallway, bathroom on one side, bedroom on the other, then opens into a large living area with a kitchen in one corner and big view of the city through a huge window.

"It's more than big enough for me," Luxana says, though I didn't offer an opinion. "After all, I don't ever plan to share it with anyone."

"That's a little defeatist, isn't it?" I ask. "I mean, there's always the chance—"

"I'm ace, Eli, so it's not an issue. And I enjoy solitude."

"Oh, sorry. I shouldn't presume."

"The fuck is ace?" Alvin says, twisting his features like he smelled something bad.

"It means asexual," Luxana says. "I lack any sexual attraction to other people."

It takes me a second to realize she just answered Alvin directly. She's even looking at him. With various yelps of "Fuck!" and "Holy shit!" my ghosts all blink out, but Luxana shoots a hand forward and closes her fist, like she's grabbing at the empty air.

"What the fuck, man?" Alvin is writhing on the spot, twisting left and right, looking down at his chest with an expression of pain and horror. The others have vanished.

"I assume you want me to help get rid of these bad spirits for you?" Luxana says, tightly gripping the air in front of her.

Alvin stills, gasping, terror in his eyes.

"Can you do that?" I ask.

"Of course." She makes a gesture with the other hand, says something under her breath as she closes her eyes for a moment. Then she pops her eyes open again, looking right at Alvin. A moment of concentration, of strenuous effort, passes her features.

"Wait a sec—" I start to say, but don't get it out before Alvin screams. He bursts apart like smoke hit with a sudden gust and his voice trails away into nothing. I feel a moment of emptiness in my chest, a sensation of drag, then it passes.

"He's gone," Luxana says with a smile. "I can pull the others back too, and do the same to them, but now you've seen the proof, we need to discuss payment."

"You killed him?" I ask stupidly. He's definitely gone. I don't know how I can tell, but I can. He's disappeared, forever and always. Shit, I almost miss him in a way. I guess I got used to the five of them.

"Killed him? He's been dead a long time, Eli. These spirits, they're hooked into you, tightly bound. You've carried this burden for a while, I can see that much. It's not a healthy way for you to live, especially bonds this strong. But the bonds can be broken."

Shit, he's really gone. I could be rid of them. All of them. But then other thoughts rattle through my mind.

Duck! Michael in the alley.

My grandma used to tell the tales, some people can scry. Sly telling me about seers.

Shoppers about forty feet behind the goons. Graney, helping me time my move earlier.

Michael pushing the crystal ball off its stand.

These assholes are useful. If they are real, and not just in my head, then they give me an edge. Information, extra eyes. I can use them. Especially if they know I can get rid of them, perhaps they'll be a little more cooperative. At least, the remaining four might be. Why the hell couldn't she have got rid of that racist fuck, Dwight? It's not like I'm a big fan of any of them, except Michael, I guess, but I would have picked Dwight in a hot second if she'd given me a choice. Maybe I could still have her get rid of him and just keep Michael, Sly and Graney. Then again, if I want their help, if I want some kind of accord with them, I need to be cautious. My mind is racing, spinning, this is too much.

Luxana smiles at me and it lights up her face. "Quite the dilemma, eh?"

"Yeah." I can't help but laugh. "This is a truly weird day."

"Well, I'm here if you decide to use my services. And seriously, it's not good for you in the long run to trail spirits behind you like this."

"What will happen?"

"Hard to know, there are various possibilities. Usually some form of psychosis settles in. Having said that, these ones around you are far more stable than usual."

I laugh again. "Stable? I don't know about that!"

"Not psychologically. More bonded to you, more readily apparent. You converse with them freely?"

"Pretty much."

"Hmm. Maybe you can live with them then. Your choice. But like I said, if you need me." She rubs thumb and fingers together in the universal gesture for 'Show me the money'.

"I need to pay you for the job you already did. I mean, I didn't ask for it or anything, but I guess it is a service provided."

"Consider it a free trial. I know you'll come back if you decide to…change your situation further."

"As it happens, you can help me right now, with something else. And I'll gladly pay for that." I pull out my cell phone, open up the picture of the signet ring and hand it over. "Do you recognize this?"

Luxana's body stiffens and the lightness of her smile vanishes. She hands the phone back immediately. "Why?"

"You clearly do recognize it."

"I want nothing to do with these people. Are they looking for you?"

My pause is all the information she needs.

"Get out, right now. Go far away. I'll meet you at Mario's Italian Restaurant in Spring Valley, tonight at eight. You make a reservation. Never come here again. I won't have them aware of my place." She pushes past me and hustles down the hall, opens the door.

Her urgency is clear despite the forced calm. I nod once. "Thank you."

I leave the apartment and take the stairs rather than wait for an elevator. When I reach the street I jog away from the building, putting as much space between myself and Luxana as quickly as possible. I'm fairly confident she'll show up for the meeting, she strikes me as honorable. My thoughts are tumbling with all that's happened.

"What the actual fuck, man?" Sly is trotting alongside me.

I look to either side. There's Michael and Dwight on my left, Sly and Graney on the right. No sign of Alvin. "He's really gone, huh?" I ask.

"Jesus, dude, she ripped him to atoms," Michael says.

"Where did he go?"

"We don't know," Graney says. "But wherever it is, there's no coming back."

I laugh. "So I could do that to any of you. I could do it to all of you."

"Why the fuck couldn't she destroy this racist asshole?" Sly asks, pointing across me at Dwight. I sympathize.

They all look contrite, and more scared than ever. And angry. "Tell you what," I say. "I'll keep you all around if you agree to help me. Stop fucking with me and actually help."

I feel something passing between them, some reluctant agreement. They are pissed, but more than that they're terrified. This might not last, but right now I have them all on the ropes.

"Agreed?" I ask.

"Yeah," they all mutter.

I slow to a brisk walk and keep moving back toward the city. It feels like the start of a brand new day.

EIGHT

I MESSAGE BRIDGET AND SHE AGREES to meet up for a late lunch after all. The ghosts are conspicuous by their absence, no doubt licking their wounds. I can't get used to the idea that Alvin Crake is gone. The five of them have been hanging around me for a long time. And it makes me wonder again, why those five? I killed a lot of folks over the years, and more than a few would have considered their execution unjust. Maybe something to ask Luxana later. Is five the limit? Will a new one move in? You see, this is why I'm so discontented. Too many fucking questions. Another hovering around me like a bad smell is this: How long before Santiago tracks me down again? The first time he only brought two heavies, the second time he brought five. I can't help thinking he'll show up with an army next.

"You look serious."

I startle slightly, realize I was lost in my thoughts and didn't see Bridget come in. She sits opposite me in the booth and takes my hand over the table.

"You okay?" she asks.

I allow a crooked smile. "That obvious, huh?"

"What's happening?"

Man, how much do I tell her? How much will she accept? Will it drive her away? Again with all the questions. I wish I could just return the ring to Santiago and forget all about it, but he won't let it go now, not after losing so many of his men. And besides, I need to know. My curiosity puts cats to shame.

I take a deep breath, then, "Let's order some food, and then I have a lot to tell you."

Bridget keeps quiet while we order burgers and shakes, tells me about her day as we wait for them to arrive. "I'm doing great," she says. "I'll be ready to blow this place before long. Honestly, I think I have to anyway. I'm getting noticed."

The food arrives and the waitress smiles as she puts it down, then turns away without a word.

"So, what is it?" Bridget says. "I feel like you're about to break up with me. You meet someone else?"

"Holy shit, no! I'm worried you'll quit me when I get through telling you some stuff."

"I'm sure it's not that bad, Eli."

I stare into her beautiful eyes for a moment and she looks right back, unperturbed. She's strong, confident, assured of herself. It's one of her most attractive features. And she's smart, another damned sexy trait. I guess I need to be as honest as I can.

"Okay, it's like this. Those guys I ran into the other night? I took something from one of them. A ring. No big deal. It was gold, looked valuable. I thought it might be worth something and I figured I'd earned it, you know?"

Bridget shrugs, nods, keeps chewing.

"Well, turns out the ring belongs to someone and it has some kind of… I don't know, this'll sound hokey, but it has some kind of magic about it and the people I took it from can track it."

Bridget laughs. "Magic? Computer chip, dummy."

My turn to shrug. "Maybe, but I don't think so. Anyway, the guy who came after it wasn't the guy I took it from, so there's a group at work here. I don't know any more than that."

"And you're disinclined to return the ring and be done with it?"

"I may have caused some collateral damage because they didn't ask nicely. So, I think we're past the return and forget stage."

Bridget stares at me, swallows, but doesn't take another bite. I cover my discomfort by eating some of my own lunch. "And you wanna know," Bridget says. It's not a question. "You're a little bored mooching around while I make the big bucks, you're used to a little action and mayhem, and you feel kinda like maybe you want to run up against these guys and have some fun. Am I close?"

I can't help laughing. "Pretty much a bullseye."

"Eli." She shakes her head, but a soft smile is tugging one side of her mouth. "Okay, so maybe hide the ring somewhere so they can't find you and learn a little more first."

She's good. "I did exactly that. Trouble is, they found me again even without the ring."

Her eyebrow pops up and then she frowns. "How?"

"I wish I knew."

"This is why you said magic? You really believe in that stuff?"

I swallow, mind racing. I love Bridget, I think I have to admit that. I want her around, and that means honesty. Relationships only work when there are no lies. I need to take a chance here. "Magic's not the right word. But supernatural, maybe? You believe in anything like that?"

Bridget nods. "Yeah, a little. There's a lot of bullshit out there, but there's also a lot of stuff we don't understand. It's arrogant to think we know everything. My grandma was a bit psychic, she'd get premonitions and stuff."

"Really?"

"Sure. There's this story that when my mom was a kid, maybe four years old, she was playing outside. The family had a house and garden, big fish pond at the end of a long backyard. My grandma is busy in the kitchen when she suddenly goes cold and yells, "She's drowning!" and runs to the door. My grandfather was gardening, and Grandma comes running along yelling, "She's drowning!" and they both start sprinting to the end of the yard, and there's my mom, drifting face down in the fish pond. She went in after a ball and slipped out of her depth. My grandfather hauled her out, managed to revive her. Another few minutes and she'd have been dead."

"Holy shit."

Bridget smiles. "Yeah. Neither of them could see her from where they were, but somehow Grandma knew. There's a bunch of stories like that about Grandma. And I'm pretty sure I saw a ghost once."

"Really?" Now I'm starting to relax. This might be easier than I thought.

"Yeah, haunted house out near Hollywood when I worked for Jerry. There was a private game there, we stayed a couple of nights. This old lady, all in white, used to walk the halls. I asked about her and the owner said she died there in eighteen hundred and something. Only a few people ever see her."

"Well, how about that."

"So, you think there's something supernatural about this ring? Ghosts and premonitions are one thing, but what you're describing is a bit of a stretch."

I nod, chewing more burger. "Yeah, I get it. But there's something else. There's something supernatural about me."

"You?"

"Michael, you there?"

Bridget frowns at me, but stays quiet, patient.

I'm about to ask again when Michael says, "What's up?"

He's sitting right next to me in the booth, the blown-open side of his face not a foot from me, glistening with blood, dripping onto his shoulder, bone fragments stark white against the fluorescents of the diner. "That thing you did with the crystal ball?"

"Yeah?"

I gesture at the table in front of us.

Michael sighs. "You want to show her we're real now that *you* don't doubt us anymore, that it?"

"Yep."

"Who are you talking to?" Bridget says tightly. "You're freaking me out, Eli."

I smile at her. "I'm really sorry. But this is me and I love you and I need you to know."

She's a little open-mouthed at that, and maybe I shouldn't but I find it sexy as hell. Shocking her is fun. I glance at Michael, raise an eyebrow. Graney, Sly and Dwight are lined up behind the booth, looking over Bridget, scowling.

"You know, it's really hard to do this," Michael says. "And it hurts like hell when I do. I never feel anything anymore, except when I try to interact like this and that's agony." He looks up at the other three ghosts. "They can't do it at all, they say, but I don't know if they ever tried."

"Please?" I ask. "Just a little."

Bridget is seriously uncomfortable now, looking at me like I'm mad.

Michael sighs. He reaches out, his fingertips near my water glass.

I sit back, make sure my hands are far out of the way and say to Bridget, "Watch the glass."

Michael lets out a moan of pain through gritted teeth and the glass slides about six inches across the table toward Bridget. Michael fades out and Bridget gasps.

"What the fuck? Did you do that?"

"No. I have… There are a few ghosts who hang around me all the time, and one of them can do that. His name is Michael."

She stares at me, dumbfounded. Seems like she's been doing a lot of that since lunch started. She goes to speak a couple of times before she finds the words. "How long have they been with you."

"Few years."

"And they're always there?"

"Kinda. They come and go a bit, but yeah."

"How many?"

"Four." Seems strange to say that now. No new number five yet, anyway.

"Always the same four?"

"Yep."

"Wow. Okay. Fuck me."

"Okay?"

Bridget laughs. "Well, what else is there? I mean, if they've always been around since I met you, and you're telling me now, but I haven't noticed before, then I guess not much really changes, right?"

The relief that washes through me is palpable. I don't know if this will last, but it's a better first stage than I anticipated. "I hope so. I really hope so, Bridget."

"You love me, huh?"

"That didn't slip by you then."

She smiles, super sultry. But she doesn't say it back. I can see the mischief in her eyes. I don't want her to say it if she doesn't mean it. After what I've just shown her, I don't blame her for staying a little reticent. "And why *are* you telling me now?" she asks.

"Well, mainly because I think you deserve to know. Honesty, yeah? But also because I think whatever this is I'm mixed up in, it has something unnatural about it."

"Supernatural."

"Yeah."

"Shit, Eli. Maybe we should just go. We can. I have enough. I was going to play a few more days, but we can call it early if you want."

"No, thanks. I want to learn more. I feel… I dunno, kinda compelled to see more of all this. And that's the other reason I told you about this stuff. I found someone today who knows more. She's got crazy supernatural skills. Honestly, I was pretty shocked. And she's agreed to help me, so I'm meeting her later. The ring has a kind of symbol carved on it and she didn't like it at all, told me to get away from her place and meet her later. So that's what I'm doing at eight. Okay?"

"I guess. I have a game starting at nine, so no sweat there. She? Do I need to be concerned?"

I remember Luxana talking directly to Alvin before she wiped him out. *It means asexual. I lack any sexual attraction to other people.* And I wouldn't cheat on Bridget anyway, not for anything. "No, you definitely don't need to worry at all."

Bridget nods, eating her food and thinking. Eventually she looks up and says, "Okay, but a couple of caveats. One, you don't take unnecessary risks. Two, you get me and we run if things get too weird. Three, no more secrets, even by omission. We owe each other total transparency, yeah?"

"Yeah. Okay."

"I'll be honest, Eli, I don't like this. I want it on the record here and now that my preference is to pack up and leave. You're freaking me out more than a little."

"I get that, and I'm sorry. But even if I wanted to, I think maybe Santiago could track me anywhere now, so perhaps I *need* to see this through."

She sighs. "Damn it, Eli. Be careful, okay?"

"Always."

NINE

MARIO'S ITALIAN RESTAURANT is a nice place. Nothing fancy, but spacious, well-decorated. The smell as I walk in is fantastic. A *maître'd* meets me and asks my name.

"Corleone," I say. "Table for two, eight o'clock."

It's ten minutes to, but I wanted to be sure I was here before Luxana.

If the *maître'd* suspects my cheesy fake name, he doesn't show it. "Your table is ready. This way."

It's in the back of the wide space, a small square table up against the wall, chairs either side. A good spot. A candle burns in a glass bulb in the center, cutlery and napkins neatly laid out. The tablecloths are all deep red, the chairs dark wood, the walls an off-white. The net effect is one of soft privacy despite the open room. Good choice by Luxana. I order a drink and pretend to study the menu while I watch the door from the corner of my eye. I hope she shows. I started to wonder if maybe she wouldn't, but then again, if she didn't show up she can only expect me to go back to her place to find out why. Which I would do. And I know she doesn't want that. My other concern is that Santiago has been conspicuous by his absence. I feel like he might show up at any moment, and that bothers me.

Michael, Graney, Sly and Dwight are sitting around a table next to mine, lounging in the chairs, scowling at me. I raise an eyebrow at them.

"Thought we might see what this bitch had to say," Graney says.

"Not scared she'll…" I grab the air then flick my fingers open.

"Yeah, that's exactly what we're scared of, cocheese. But you made us a promise."

I suppose I did, but I won't sit here talking to myself where the other diners can see, so I just nod and smile.

"You better keep the promise, Eli," Michael says.

My turn to raise an eyebrow at him.

"Yeah, yeah, and we'll help whenever we can."

"We won't fucking like it," Graney says. "Don't expect too much or maybe we'll take our chances."

I offer a small shrug at that and they go back to scowling.

"This woman, she's way more than Papa Night," Sly says. "And you remember the crazy shit he got up to. Watch yourself with her."

I nod again and notice Luxana arrive at the door. She looks directly at me, then her eyes flick to the table with the ghosts and she frowns. There's a moment of conversation with the *maitre'd* and she points at me. He smiles and walks her over. She ignores the ghosts completely, offers me a pleasant smile and sits down.

"Thanks for coming," I say. "I really appreciate it."

"Best way to keep you away from my place."

"Yeah, that's what I thought."

She casts a glance at the ghosts and then back to me. "Decided to live with them?"

"Yeah, for now. I know so much more already."

"Right. Well, in that case, you can use them."

"Okay."

A waiter comes over, so we order wine and food. I let her choose the wine, and she orders a carbonara while I pick spaghetti and meatballs.

When the waiter leaves again, she says, "Okay, ground rules. One, you pay for dinner and give me a thousand bucks flat payment, no negotiation. Can you afford that?"

"A thousand bucks? Fuck that bitch!" Dwight says.

She turns a glare to him and he blanches and pops out, just vanishes. The other three remain, but look scared.

"I think he forgot you can see us," Graney says. "Hear us."

"He has very little in this department," Sly says, tapping the side of his head with one index finger.

"I can afford it," I say, to bring us back to the important stuff.

Luxana looks back to me and nods. "Number two, after tonight, we're finished. You don't contact me again, for any reason. If you're involved with these people, I want nothing to do with you."

"I plan to get uninvolved."

"I don't think that's possible, but best of luck. I'll give you all the tools I can, but it won't be much."

"Okay."

She pours water for us both from the decanter on the table and sips from hers. Then she looks up. "You don't have that ring on you, right?"

"No. But they can still find me without it."

She nods, glances at the big windows of the restaurant. "They probably won't challenge you in here, but maybe when you leave."

"I thought the same. I'll leave first in case they're out there."

"Yes, you will."

"Who are they?"

"The Acolytes of Ur."

My brain spins for a moment as I try to process that. She lets me think. Eventually, I say, "Okay, so Ur was a Sumerian city? In Mesopotamia?" Yeah, I'm a well-read motherfucker, I know some stuff.

She smiles. "Still is a city. And yes, it was an important city-state, dates from about 3,800 BCE."

"And an acolyte assists a priest or something, right? That name doesn't really make sense."

"It does if you believe what these assholes believe. An acolyte can assist a priest in the modern sense, sure, but they can also be the hands on Earth of a god. This group, they believe that Ur the city was founded by the moon god Nanna. They think the moon *is* a god, or at least the corporeal representation of the moon god for us on Earth. They believe the god sent a piece of itself to Earth and it landed and became the city of Ur. You've heard of the Ziggurat of Ur? They believe it's a temple built to revere the moon good, Nanna. But all this is twisted mythology and kind of irrelevant. The main point is that they claim to serve a moon god who is in turn a gateway to cosmic powers beyond the ken of mortal beings like us lowly humans. They are the acolytes of that force here."

"Acolytes of Ur," I say quietly. "I mean, I guess Acolytes of Nanna would sound pretty lame."

Luxana laughs, and it's a high, pleasant sound. "Right? It's an unfortunate word in English, but don't let logic or anything like that get in the way of religious beliefs." She becomes serious again. "Don't underestimate them." She gestures at my ghosts, and I notice Dwight is back, loitering a bit farther away now. "You know these spirits are real," Luxana says. "You saw what I did to one of them."

I nod.

"You miss him? Wish I hadn't done that?"

"He's not the one I would have picked if you'd given me a choice. But I can get used to it."

"Good. So you know they're here and you know I'm the real deal, so you should be open to anything I might tell you. So, listen when I tell you this. However hokey the Acolytes of Ur might sound, they are dangerous and genuinely powerful. They're a cabal, essentially, of some of the most rich and powerful men and women in the country and they do whatever they like. They get away with anything. And they do it for power. Corruption in politics, pedophile rings, snuff movies, all that horrible shit. They prey on people for shits and giggles. They simply crave power. They gain favor through the moon god from the cosmic entities beyond. It's real, it's powerful, and you should have fuck all to do with it."

"Too late for that, I think." What she just said only makes me want to hurt them more.

"Extricate yourself if you can. I suggest you return the ring somehow, and slip away. They'll be able to find the ring if you leave it somewhere accessible. Do that and leave town. Maybe leave the country, in fact. They might let you go." Her eyes narrow. "Why haven't they taken the ring back already?"

"I hid it in a silver case, tucked away safe."

"Okay, makes sense. How did you know to do that?"

I tip my head sideways at the gathered assholes, now all four sitting at the table again, watching intently. They're quiet and well-behaved, for the first time ever. I like this new compliance.

"Smart," Luxana says. "But I don't know how long that'll last. It masks well, but not forever. Not something that powerful."

I feel a moment of fear for Stanley and hope he's okay. That should be my next job. If the ring isn't really safe there, I need to get it away from him. He has enough of his own troubles. "How many are in this cabal?" I ask.

Luxana shakes her head. "I don't know. In Vegas, at least a dozen, maybe more. Across the country?" She shrugs. "Maybe hundreds. Who knows? Across the world, maybe more."

"But it's the ones here I need to worry about?"

"I guess. I have no idea how much they all talk to each other. Really, Eli, just get away from them all."

Our food arrives and we're quiet for a moment while the waiter offers us pepper and parmesan. We eat a little in silence once the waiter leaves again. The food is really good.

"I've never seen spirits as realized as yours," Luxana says suddenly.

"Really?"

"Getting rid of that one, breaking his bond, that was the hardest I've ever had to work."

"They came to me in a period of…" I run out of words. What the hell do I call the breakdown that happened after Caitlin and Scottie died?

"Must have been some extreme trauma," Luxana says. "Spirits tend to gain a hold when a person is both traumatically compromised and their mind is open to corruption. It's a fairly unique set of circumstances, and even then a person might get caught by one spirit, usually a weak bond. You had five, and bonded like nothing I've ever seen before. And those four are still so strong."

"My situation was pretty unique back then." Something occurs to me. "So, I won't get any more?"

"Not likely, without a similar set of circumstances. But anything is possible in this world. These happened to be around you at the right time. I imagine you're stuck with those four alone, though. Unless you want me to—"

"Not right now, thanks. We've got an understanding." I feel like I've learned a lot, and there's some solace in understanding the situation a little better.

"In that case, you can use them to stop the cabal finding you. In the short term, at least." She glances at the ghosts. "If they agree?"

"They better," I say, looking over at them too. "That's part of our agreement."

"We'll do what we can," Michael says. The others look annoyed, but don't contradict him.

Luxana looks back to me. "Okay, so this is how it works. The Acolytes can find you because they've met you. Everyone has a kind of psychic signature, like a dog always knows another person's scent, yes?"

I nod. "Sly said something similar. Hi grandma called them seers."

"Good enough a name. A strong seer can always find another person's psychic resonance. It's a skill some people develop. It's not common, it's very hard to do, but some folks have got good at it. If they stopped being able to track you by the ring you showed me a picture of, they would start using that method instead assuming one of them had met you."

"Yeah, and I met him right back with a barstool. So that's how they found me again after I hid the ring."

"Exactly. But you can muddy the scent for them, because you have those spirits. You need to have one of them always ghosting you, always close. It won't be comfortable, I expect, but you need one of those four always pretty much on you."

"On me?"

"Yeah. Like a piggyback or something."

"Get fucked!" Dwight snaps, then blanches when Luxana looks at him.

"A piggyback?" Sly says.

Luxana grins. She's enjoying this. "You'll feel them there, but it won't really be a physical burden. I don't know how it'll feel, to be honest. But because they're dead, their psychic aura will be indistinct. And unknown to the cabal, of course. So it will kind of mess up yours. Another living person would be easily discerned, even lying on top of you, it would be two clear auras. A spirit isn't like that. It's not physically here, but energetically exists, understand?"

"I think so."

She grins again. "Imagine there's a nice-smelling rose, then someone puts a rancid old cheese under the table the rose is on. Right nearby but just out of sight. What are you gonna smell?"

"Rancid old cheese," I say, and grin too.

"Don't enjoy this too fucking much, asshole," Graney says.

"Shut up, rancid," I say, without looking at him.

I realize that in all this time, my ghosts have been around but not that close to me. Always at least a few feet away. I already know I'm not going to like their proximity, but if it works, I'll put up with it. For a little while anyway, until I've taken care of these Acolyte assholes. Despite Luxana's fears, I plan to hit them hard.

"Okay, thanks. I'll do that." I look at the ghosts. "Choose who goes first."

They make noises of annoyance and anger then start arguing among themselves.

Luxana nods at my plate. "Eat what more you want, then you

have to leave. We're done here. I'll take my time finishing my dinner, in case they're waiting for you. But I don't want them to see us together. I've already taken more of a chance than I'm comfortable with. Don't forget to pay on your way out."

The finality in her tone brooks no argument. "What about the grand in payment you wanted?"

She flaps one hand. "I don't really need that. I was just testing how serious you were about knowledge."

"Oh. Thanks."

"Don't thank me. You're in a world of shit, Eli, and I don't think you'll get out. No one who fucks with the Acolytes of Ur gets out. Good luck, but this is probably goodbye."

I can't help a small laugh. "Thanks for the vote of confidence."

She smiles, but it's half-hearted and entirely humorless. "Sorry."

I cram another couple of forkfuls of food, then stand up. "Thanks, really. I appreciate it."

She nods and I feel her watching as I leave. I pay and the *maitre'd* asks if everything is okay.

"All fine, thanks," I tell him. "Make sure my friend enjoys her dinner and gets any dessert or drinks she wants, okay?" I put another hundred on the counter. "And anything left over is for you."

The *maitre'd* smiles and inclines his head. "Thank you, sir. You have a good night, now."

"You too."

I leave, but something tells me my night is not going to be good at all.

TEN

As I STEP OUT THE RESTAURANT DOOR, Michael says, "Hood up."

I don't second guess the request, just pull my cap low over my eyes and put my hood over it.

"Stop in that doorway," Graney says.

I glance toward the curb and see him pointing at a darkened shop entry just up the street.

"Quickly," Michael says.

Nice to see these assholes are taking their new helpful role seriously. Without any delay I duck into the shadows and press myself into the corner.

"Ride him like a fucking piggyback," Sly says. He's leaning on the wall just outside this recessed entry, sucking on a joint. Dwight is next to him and Sly even shares his joint with the racist. He truly is distracted.

"Who am I hiding from?" I ask.

"Santiago is just down the street," Michael says, pointing. "He didn't see you come out, but he knows you're here. I don't think he knows who with, probably doesn't care. He's waiting for you."

"One of his goons strolled by the restaurant while you were jawin' with Luxana," Sly says. "Clocked you in there and reported back. I think maybe they didn't expect you to leave so soon."

Hopefully that goon won't remember enough about Luxana to compromise her. I was just having dinner with a lady friend. "How many?" I ask.

"There are two cars up ahead," Michael says. "A black sedan and a white SUV, both with four people inside. So that's seven plus Santiago."

Graney nods back the other way. "Two more cars down there, a pair of Jeep Cherokees, with another eight people."

"Sixteen mooks this time." I can't help thinking that's more of a challenge.

"How much ammo you got, sucker?" Graney asks.

I always used to use a Glock 19. It's what Vern preferred and he was the one who brought me up in the life. And it's a good weapon. But I'm a fucking good shot, supernaturally good some people have said, but shooting is just something that always came naturally to me. Plus, I put in a shit ton of practice. Now recently, with Bridget at the tables so much, I've had time on my hands. So I've been down the range plenty, putting in more practice. A guy there introduced me to the CZ 75 9mm. Man, it's a sweet pistol. The guy at the range called it a Czechmate, seeing as it's made in the Czech Republic and it always wins. I've come to find it much more comfortable. Which is all a long way of saying, I have twenty rounds immediately accessible, ten in each mag of the two CZ 75s I have concealed. I have another two mags, one tucked in each pocket. Honestly, even someone as paranoid as me should think forty available rounds across two weapons would be plenty for general self-defense, right? But then, not many people get sixteen mooks sent after them.

"Plenty of ammo," I say. I should be able to drop sixteen assholes without needing my second mags if the situation was right. But it's not. A big group to either side, wide open sidewalk, a fairly busy road right beyond that and buildings all along this side, I'm pretty hemmed in. I just need to get away. If I can end Santiago during my exit, I will.

"They didn't see me come out?" I ask Michael. "You're sure?"

"Pretty sure. You weren't on the sidewalk more than two seconds."

"If they did see you, they're not doing anything about it," Graney says.

"What *is* happening?"

Graney shrugs. "Nothin'. They're sitting in their cars like idiots." He looks up the street each way, shrugs again.

"Okay," I say. "Here's where we all start working together. No point in trying out this thing Luxana suggested as they know I'm here. I need to get away, then start carrying one of you pricks around with me. Getting away is the key part. What can any of you do to help?"

"We cain't do jack shit, cocheese. Michael seems to be able to exert like about a mouse's fart of pressure in the world, but that's it. We can tell you shit, but about all I gotta tell ya is that you're about to fuckin' die."

"You're a fucking idiot," I say. Graney, Michael and Sly all say exactly the same thing. We even manage to share a laugh about that. Look at us all working as a team suddenly.

"Fuck all a'y'all!" Dwight says, and fades out.

"He's chucking a temper tantrum?" I say. "Guess we won't miss him."

"He'll be back," Sly says.

"You reckon Santiago is the seer?" I ask Sly. "He's the one tracking me down?"

"Yeah, must be. But that doesn't mean he's the only one. Who knows how many of these fuckers there are."

"Good point. But if I can take out Santiago, it'll level the field at least a little."

"Take him out?" Michael says. "From here?"

"You tell me which one he is, and yeah. Then I pop as many of the heavies as I can and fucking run. Honestly, I can't think of a better plan really. They're going to jump me the moment they see me, right?"

"Almost certainly," Graney says.

"Okay, well as you lot are useless for anything physical, let's at least get some reconnaissance. I need to know what weapons they have, what else they have, maybe what they're talking about. And which one is Santiago."

They all stare at me.

"Well? You helping now or what? Scram. Get me info!"

"Fuck me," Graney says, and stomps away toward the Jeeps back down the street. Michael and Sly head for the cars farther up.

It's an anxious few minutes. I want so badly to stick my head out of the shadows, take a look, check the street. Anything other than just standing in the dark waiting. But this concealment is the only advantage I have.

"Santiago is in the front passenger seat of the second car up there, the black sedan," Michael says, suddenly right beside me in the shadows. "The SUV in front of his has four goons, two armed with semi-automatic pistols and two have a shotgun each. The sedan has a guy in the driver's seat with a 9mm, Santiago beside him, without a weapon I could see. In the back are two more with Glocks."

"Pretty much the same configuration in the Jeeps back there," Graney says, jerking a thumb back over his shoulder. Except one extra gun. From what I can see, six 9mm pistols, two shotguns."

"So that's four shotguns and eleven 9mms at least. Fucking hell, that's some pretty heavy firepower."

Graney raises an eyebrow at me. "For just little old you. Pretty impressive."

"I think there's a way to cause enough mayhem to get you away," Michael says. At my look, he continues. "In the SUV, one of the guys in the back seat has his shotgun resting across his lap, but it's pointing toward the front. If it went off, it would kill at least one, if not both the mooks in the front seats."

I smile. "Now we're talking, my friend. You think you could pull that trigger?"

"I think so. If I had to."

"And I could take out at least a couple from the sedan before they started moving. Maybe even Santiago too."

"Timing," Sly says.

"What?"

"You're taking a hell of a gamble. It's all down to timing. And those assholes in the Jeeps will be out and after you in moments."

I run it through my mind a couple of times, then say, "Okay, but they still think I'm in the restaurant. I can buy a few seconds by starting here and a few seconds is a long time in a gunfight. I'll get away from the two cars behind, toward the mayhem, before they can really get moving." I shift back in the shadows and try to see down the street to catch a glimpse of the cars. I can just see a black corner of a sedan without giving up my cover. I describe it.

"Yep, that's the one Santiago is in," Michael says.

I try to build the picture in my mind's eye, imagining the dimensions of the car, the positions of the occupants. If a shotgun goes off in the car ahead of Santiago, their attention will be that way and I can surely shoot at least a couple. Then I wing it.

"Okay, let's do this. Michael, you get in position, Sly you stand by that sedan so you can see Michael. Graney, you stay here on the sidewalk by me. When Michael is ready, Sly signals you, you signal me. I say go, you drop your hand, Sly drops his, Michael booms the shotgun. Same moment, I pop out and take out whoever I can, hopefully including Santiago. I'll run right for those cars while I do it. With any luck, by the time the guys behind us know anything is going down, I'll already be moving well beyond them. As soon as I can, I'll lose myself in the traffic and run for it."

"We're all gonna fucking die," Sly says.

"You're already dead. Let's go, before they decide to check on me again."

"One other thing," Michael says.

"What?"

"Santiago was talking when I checked on them before. He was saying to his goons to make sure you're good and dead. He said, 'No questions, no pause, just kill this motherfucker.' So they don't care about the ring anymore."

A chill goes through me at that thought, but I can't spare it any time right now. "Whatever. Let's go."

Michael fades out, Sly walks away. Graney stands on the sidewalk looking down toward the cars.

"And what do I do, cocheese?"

"Suck your own asshole, for all I care."

Graney raises a hand. I draw my CZ 75s and take a long, deep breath. The adrenaline starts to surge, and breathing is the only thing that helps to mitigate the effects. Here we go. "Ready," I say.

Graney drops his hand, there's a muffled boom from up ahead, but I'm already moving. I step out, legs apart, and start firing. A gun in each hand, barking in alternating rhythm. Two heads in the back of the sedan burst, scarlet spraying black in the night as the window shatters. I fire more, aiming hard for the front passenger seat in the hope of nailing Santiago, but it's mayhem already. I take off running as someone falls out of the rear passenger door of the first car and the driver's door of the second opens. Whoever stumbled from the SUV was too distracted by the horrors inside to even look down the street and I drop him with a couple of quick rounds. That's three out of eight up there, maybe one or two more from the shotgun thanks to Michael.

There's screaming and shouting from all around, tires are screeching as cars going by skid to a halt or try to peel away from the sudden gunfight. A crash and tinkle of broken glass from collisions right beside me. I can smell gasoline and gun oil and gunpowder. The driver of Santiago's car twists up in the gap between the car body and the door he opened, the glint of a muzzle in front of him. I dive to one side as the gun barks. I glimpse the muzzle flash, but don't feel the burn of a bullet, then I'm tucking and rolling off the curb.

The goons are only about twenty paces away, and I have no idea if the eight from the Jeeps behind are tracking me yet, but I have to move. Gritting my teeth, bracing for impact, I roll onto my feet and bolt out into the road. There's a high screech of rubber and a bright red Corvette is coming right at me, fishtailing as it brakes. It won't quite stop in time, but that's okay. I jump, plant one boot on the long, smooth, shiny hood, feel it dent beneath my toes as I launch off and drop down the other side.

"What the fuck?" I hear through the open driver's window, but I have no time to explain.

I pop up, fire a few shots at random into the cars waiting for me. I catch a glimpse of Santiago in the passenger seat of the second one, face sprayed with blood, his mouth twisting in a grimace of agony. Clearly hurt, but he might not be dying.

I take an extra fraction of a second to line up, then squeeze off a shot and his head whips sideways and out of sight, a fountain of blood jetting up. Fuck you, buddy. Bullets ping off the Corvette and I hit the ground again. Those shots came from back near the Jeeps, so those boys are finally moving.

"Fucking run!" Graney screams at me, but strangely enough I was already thinking that.

Doubled over I scurry away from the Corvette and slip between two more cars, both stopped in the middle of the lane, wide-eyed drivers behind their windshields. More bullets fly and one of the drivers ducks away as their windshield shatters, then I'm past and around those cars too. I pump my arms, pump my legs, sprint hard. Every chance I get, I duck and weave, left and right, putting more vehicles between me and the goons. There's a side street off to my left and I run across into it.

"The Jeeps are giving chase," Michael says.

I sprint hard along the side street, then see a car pull up to the next intersection. Sorry about this, whoever you are. I pull open the driver's door and a young man, maybe twenty years old, looks up in shock.

"The hell, man?"

I drag him out and notice, thankfully, he has no other passengers. Against his protests, I jump in and power away, make a right at the next intersection.

"Those Jeeps just made the turn," Graney says. "They saw the kid sitting in the road, but they didn't see what car you got in."

I slow to a more normal driving speed and start heading back toward the city, watching my mirror hard. Eventually I say, "Looks like I lost them."

"Can't believe you got away with that," Graney says.

"All about surprise and timing," I say. "Never underestimate either in a fight." I turn to Michael, in the passenger seat. "Good work with the shotgun."

"Blew away the front passenger," Michael says.

Graney, Sly and Dwight are all lined up in the back.

"Killed by a dead guy," Sly says with a laugh. "How embarrassing."

"It's a useful skill you have there, Michael. Why can you do it?"

"I don't know. Just can."

I glance in the rearview mirror. "You three should practice or some shit. Would be good if you could all do it."

ELEVEN

I DRIVE THE POOR GUY'S CAR about halfway back home, then park it neatly at the curb.

"Wish I could think of a way to get this back to him," I say, as I wipe all my prints off it.

The fob has only the car key and one other on it, probably his home. I lock up, drop the keys in a drain. He'll get the car back, once he reports it missing. It'll get found soon enough. Hopefully he has spares. I set off in a brisk walk back toward the Strip.

"Now where?" Michael asks me.

"First, did you guys decide who rides first?"

"Ah, fuck, man!" Sly says. "You shot Santiago in the head."

"Yeah, but we don't know that he's the only seer. I'm not taking the chance. I'm hiding until I get these fuckers taken apart."

"Take Luxana's advice," Graney says. "Collect Bridget and get outta Dodge. Just leave the country."

I shake my head. "If they're as powerful as she says, you think they're going to ignore that I've killed a bunch of their gang? Particularly Santiago, he'd be high up. They'll come for me. I won't wait for it. Best defense is offense and all that."

"Take the chance, man!" Sly says. "They won't be organized enough to start tracking you again yet."

I flick a glance to him walking farthest away from me. "So you picked the short straw, huh?" Why else would he be so against the idea?

He grunts in annoyance. "Fucking rock, paper, god damned scissors."

"Climb aboard, big boy."

The look on his face is priceless. The other three are laughing, but I don't know what they're so happy about. They'll all get a turn.

"One hour!" Sly says. "Then we switch."

"I thought you guys had no concept of time."

Sly jabs a finger at me. "I'm talking to you! You set a timer. Every hour, you let us know and we switch."

"Okay." I set a timer on my phone, but I make it two hours. See if they notice.

"God damn it," Sly says.

He moves over behind me and as he gets close I feel a slight chill. He puts his hands on my shoulders and I barely suppress a gasp, the touch is like ice. It's as though my T-shirt and hoodie aren't even there, like dead skin pressed right against my flesh. Sly makes noises of discomfort as he climbs onto my back, but I don't feel any physical movement, just sliding frost, thick and somehow oily. I'm tempted to cup my hands behind, like giving a piggyback to a kid, but there's no point, I can't touch him. Memories of carrying Scottie like this flash through my mind, and grief is a gut punch that takes my breath away. Clenching my teeth, I push the thoughts away. Sly's body presses up against my back and the cold, oily sensation intensifies. Like someone has draped a thick, damp, greasy blanket over my back, shoulders, head. Except it's both heavy and gossamer at the same time. I can't *feel* it with nerves, but I carry the burden regardless. It feels terrible, makes me a little nauseated. Saliva gathers in my mouth like I'm going to puke and I have to gasp a few quick, deep breaths to push the compulsion down again.

"This ain't fucking natural," Sly says.

"No kidding," I mutter. "What about any of you is anything like natural?"

Michael, Graney, and Dwight are walking alongside, all half-laughing, half-appalled. It's like they're watching one of those gross-out horror movies, funny and disgusting at the same time.

There's a push-pull sensation happening, I feel like I'm about to stagger despite the lack of physical weight. The etheric weight is considerable.

"Will you fucking relax!" I hiss.

Sly grumbles some more, but I sense him taking metaphorical breaths. Despite the amount of weed he smokes, spirits don't actually breathe, do they? Everything starts to settle, Sly's presence becoming more like a mist around me than an oily cargo.

"Better," I say.

"You look different," Michael says, squinting.

Graney nods. "Not like you anymore. Like, I can see the physical you, but at the same time, you're unrecognizable. I feel like I have dementia or something."

"This is what the seer would see," Michael says. "The physical presence is there, but the ethereal is weird. Without laying actual eyes on you, you'd never be spotted."

"We need to all stay close," Graney says, face a grimace of something close to pain. "If we fade out too far, we might not find our way back to him."

"If you get lost, whoever's covering me at the time can get off for a while," I say. "But stay close in case."

"I don't like any of this," Dwight says.

I shrug. "And I don't like you, you piece of shit, but here we are."

Sly huffs a laugh right beside my ear and it's a horrible feeling. I do my best to ignore it. He's got his legs wrapped around my waist, one arm hooked around my neck. In the other is the ubiquitous joint and I smell the weed, see the bluish clouds drifting around my head.

"You be ready to lose that the moment I say," I tell him. "I can't have spirit smoke obscuring my vision if I get in trouble."

"Just say the word, man." Sly passes the joint along the line of assholes.

As we walk past a large shop window I catch a glimpse of us, four walking in a line, the fifth riding me like some giant kid at the fairground. How fucking ridiculous. At least anyone else would only see me.

I move past Planet Hollywood and head toward Stanley's café. The cold I'm feeling now isn't anything to do with Sly on my back. And I know I'm taking a chance, but I have to know. This is probably my only opportunity before they regroup.

The café is closed. I know the passcode for the keypad by the door and press the buttons. Usually when we caught up here I'd ring and Stanley would come to open the door, some semblance of normalcy. Sometimes the grief got too much for him, the melancholy making him eschew crowds, even the sight of the street. Like I said before, he was never really suited to Vegas. Those times I'd let myself in, and I'd usually arrive with an extra bottle.

I lock the door behind me and go through the dim interior. The lights are off, chairs on tables, smell of bleach and old coffee. I realize how familiar this place has become and my heart is racing when I go through into the back. It's quiet. Too quiet. I didn't even bother to ring first. When you know, you know.

I find him in the bedroom and my anger flares. Absolutely no one deserves this.

"Jesus fuck," Graney says, turning away.

"Oh," Michael says.

"That ain't something anyone deserves," Dwight says.

Sly is strangely silent. I feel like maybe he's simply not looking.

Stanley is hanging above his big king-sized bed. They've used a nail gun or something similar through his hands and arms, pinning him to the wall crucifix-style. Blood runs down the white paint in thin rivulets, making it look like he has gory wings. His head hangs, chin on his chest, eyes wide and blank, staring at the mess on the stark white sheets. They've thrown all the pillows and covers off the bed, sliced him open and dragged his entrails out to spell ELI across the smooth expanse of the bed. The way his eyes are open, I can't help feeling like he was still alive, watching them do that before shock and blood loss finished him.

The safe is right here in his room and the door stands open, the contents gone. All his cash and papers. And their fucking ring.

"Stanley, I'm sorry," I whisper.

"Too late for sorry," Stanley says.

The gasps of my ghosts match my own as I spin around. Stanley is there in the doorway to his bedroom, looking in. I can see the living room right through him, he's more insubstantial than my peanut gallery. Is he my new number five? Then I remember Luxana's explanation, that I needed to be suffering real trauma for the haunts to bond so tightly. Appallingly, this doesn't traumatize me. Saddens me, sure. Angers the fuck out of me. But that's all.

"Stan," I manage.

He flaps a hand. "Fuck it, don't worry about it. My life was a misery anyway. Fuck me, though, it hurt." He grimaces, looks away from the mess of his physical self and his gaze drilling directly into my eyes is more powerful than it ever was in life. "Just do one thing, Eli. Fucking get them for me."

"I will." And I mean it. "I most definitely will."

He nods once and turns away, walks out through his living room and fades away to nothing as he goes.

"He's gone," Michael says. "Like, permanently gone. That felt like a more gentle version of when Alvin was sent away."

I nod, turn back to the corpse. My name in pink and grey entrails makes me furious.

"This is some fucking message," Graney says.

It is. And it says a lot. Not least that they anticipated not catching me at the restaurant. Maybe they did this before Santiago tracked me down again. Regardless, it means they're taking no chances. They're telling me they know all they need to know. Then a new chill blasts through me.

Bridget!

TWELVE

"**W**HAT'S HAPPENING, ELI? You sounded so stressed on the phone."

I can never hide anything from Bridget. The Lily Bar and Lounge at the Bellagio Hotel is busy and crowded, appearing more packed than it really is with all the mirrors around the walls. We're sitting on velour couches the color of sick Caucasian skin and I'm attracting a lot of frowns for my jeans, boots and hooded top. The dress code is apparently "upscale fashionable attire" but, honestly, I don't even know what the fuck that is. I'm being tolerated because I'm with Bridget and she's a high roller. But I don't think they'll put up with me for long. That's okay, I don't need long.

"Yeah, sorry about that. I'm glad you're okay, that's all." I can only assume because she's been at the tables all day, the Acolytes haven't had a chance to get to her yet. And that worked for me. Stanley wasn't so lucky.

"Why shouldn't I be okay?"

"I can only apologize in advance, but I think I've dragged you into something really dangerous. I didn't mean to, and if I thought it would go like this, I'd have backed out well before now."

Bridget tips her head to one side. "Would you though? Really?"

I can't help a short laugh. "Maybe not. I dunno. But I am genuinely sorry."

"So, it's time to go? Where are we off to?"

"It's time for *you* to go. I have to stay and wrap this up or it might follow us."

She purses her lips, seemingly equal parts concerned and angry. As she opens her mouth to say something, my phone starts trilling an annoying repetitive tone. I silence it and look sidelong at the gang sitting around me. "Time to change it up."

"Fuck." Dwight gets up and comes over.

"Thank fuck for that," Sly says, sliding off me as Dwight climbs on. The transfer is uncomfortable. If darkness had a texture, it would feel like this. Dwight feels different to Sly which is strange. Just as cold, but a different kind of greasy. I try not to think on it too hard, just grit my teeth as the repellant changeover takes place. I can't suppress a shudder as Dwight settles in. Sly joins Graney and Michael on chairs opposite me and Bridget.

"The hell was that?" Bridget asks.

"Okay, full transparency. I'm going to tell you as much as I can. But I have to be quick and we need to talk while we're moving, yeah?"

"The apartment first. I can be packed in ten minutes."

"No, sorry, we're going directly to the airport."

"What?"

"They know everything."

"Eli, there's a fortune stashed at the apartment."

"I know, and a lot tucked away in the bank too. I'll get back the money if I can, but I think they've already got anything we left there."

Bridget's eyes flash rage. "I worked my ass off for that money, Eli."

"I know. I'm sorry. But you have your winnings from today, you have what's in the bank. I'll do all I can to recover as much as possible while I tidy this mess up. I'm sorry."

"Jesus, Eli, stop apologizing. I should have known being tied up with you would have risky side effects. If I'm honest, I did know that, and I thought it was kind of exciting. Fuck! Let's go."

I love the way she rolls with the punches.

We stay in plain sight, and stick to crowds as much as we can. If any of the Acolytes of Ur are watching us, I can't spot them. My ghosts don't see anyone either, but that doesn't mean they're not there. By the time we've got a cab and made it out to the airport, I've managed to fill Bridget in on most of what's happening. Enough that she's as keen as me to get the fuck out of Vegas. We find her a plane bound for Dallas leaving almost immediately, and I tell her to make a new flight from Dallas to somewhere well out of the US as quickly as she can. I don't want to know where. I'll contact her once I'm done with all this and find out where she went. Hopefully I'll live to get at least some of her money back to her. And hopefully she'll have me back again too, when this is over. She kisses me hard, hugs me tight while she does it. And it feels like goodbye.

My relief when she's taken off and safely in the air is physical. I told her to message me when she boards the next flight so I know she's away and safe. I won't make any moves until then. In truth, I don't know what my next move is. Somehow I have to find out a lot more about these Acolytes.

In the cab heading back to town, I try the simple approach and Google them. I'm surprised to get a bunch of hits for the name, then discover the Acolytes of Ur are a local heavy metal band. Seems a little on the nose, especially as their bass drum has the same sigil as the ring that started this whole mess.

"That's plausible deniability," Graney says.

"Is it?"

"Anyone hears about these assholes they can redirect enquiries. Tell people the Acolytes of Ur aren't real, just a dumb rock band."

"Thrash," Sly says

"What?"

"Thrash," Sly says again, nodding at my phone. "It's a style of heavy metal."

"Probably the best if you ask me," I say. I've always been a rock and blues guy, but I get down to old school thrash too. I wonder if these guys are any good.

"What the fuck ever." Graney points at the small screen. "But even so, it's a place to start. Someone connected to the band probably knows something."

"Unlikely to be the musicians though," Michael says. "My money's on their management."

Graney looks at Michael and taps his nose with one index finger, then points. "You are probably dead on there."

I really want to go to the apartment and check it out. I can only assume the Acolytes have been there already, but it would be good to know.

"Hang on," Michael says. It still freaks me out when they read my thoughts. He fades away, then a minute later he's back. "Yep, the place is gutted. They've emptied the safe and ripped through everything you own."

"Motherfuckers." Still, finding that out was easy. I have to get used to these dickheads being cooperative now. "You can just go anywhere you like?" I ask.

"Not anywhere. But you spent a lot of time in that apartment, there's a kind of resonance there. Like an echo, maybe? So, I can feel it and go there."

"Huh. Good to know."

My phone pings and I check it. Bridget has sent a text.

Leaving Dallas in 5. Leaving the US. Good luck. xxx

Damn. Even though the relief that she's away is intense, I hate that she's gone. I miss her like hell already. But I'm on my own now, and that's good given the circumstances. At least, as alone as I ever am now. The ghosts have the decency not to catch my eye.

"It's nice without Dwight around, ain't it," Sly says after a moment.

I jump slightly, but quickly realize he's still there, riding me. I start to gesture at my back and Sly grins.

"I kinda drifted off when I was up there," he says. "When our spirit mingles with yours, it's a bit like a sedative, it seems. He's out cold. I was for a lot of the time too."

"Useful. Maybe I'll leave him up there a bit longer then."

THIRTEEN

IN A STROKE OF GOOD FORTUNE, the Acolytes of Ur are playing right here in Vegas tonight, at a rock bar called Count's Vamp'd Rock Bar and Grill. Which is a weird name, but I'm just happy to keep moving forward. A net search helped me find out the band are on at 10:00 p.m., so I head into the place a little after nine. It's less than a dozen blocks from Las Vegas Boulevard, so I walked over, constantly on alert, with my hat and hoodie pulled low. I'm wearing a surprisingly convincing fake beard from a dress-up shop and a new hooded jacket and a new cap. Hopefully enough to distract a cursory eye. Hopefully the dimness of the evening and the gloom of a club will be enough to stop me being noticed if anyone there knows what I look like. But I seem to have slipped the radar for now. Too much to hope killing Santiago has somehow handicapped the whole group, but I bought a little time. I'll take what I can get. With any luck I'll learn enough quickly enough to hit them while they're reeling.

This piggybacking my ghosts thing appears to be working. It's amazing how quickly I'm becoming used to the greasy presence over my head, neck and back. I feel like I need a shower, but I also know one wouldn't help. Graney is in place right now, and man, he made more fuss than the others about it. I have to admit, I'm enjoying their discomfort.

Count's Vamp'd is kinda cool. It's a decent-sized building standing by itself in a parking lot parallel to West Sahara Avenue. Single-story, a red brick corner entrance in otherwise white walls, with a big black semi-circle awning. A sign above declares the name in vamp-ish script.

Inside it's high and open, the ceiling painted black. It smells of greasy food and beer and sweat, Metallica hammering from the sound system. The stage is not huge, silver metal lighting rigs crisscrossing only a few feet above the heads of the musicians, but they've had some mega names here over the years. The walls are purple with cartoonish guitars and music notes and other décor mounted on them. At the bar end are tables with high chairs around them, and there are booths with cobweb designs pressed into the seats around the sides. The lights above the tables are made from drums hanging on chains. Around the walls are glass display cases full of skulls and instruments, clothing and memorabilia, even motorcycles. The cobweb motif is everywhere. I immediately like the place.

I find a table near a back corner where I can see the stage, the bar, and most of the open auditorium. The place is busy already, and filling up fast. I order a beer and, as I haven't eaten since the rushed half a plate of meatballs earlier, I order a steak and fries too.

As the crowd increases, I keep an eye out for anyone who looks like something other than a regular punter. There's a lot of long hair and denim and leather and tattoos, but a lot of slacks and polo shirts too. It's obvious there's a certain percentage who are here for the thrill of visiting an iconic location, even though they really aren't especially into the rock scene. But among them all, I can't pick out anyone who might be a genuine acolyte. Then again, what would one look like?

The food is good and beer goes down well, but I only have the one. I can't afford to dull my reaction time right now. The band takes the stage at 10:00 p.m. sharp, to a huge cheer from the crowd. Looks like they're local favorites.

I have to admit, they're pretty good. Fast and hard riffs, double-kick drums like machine-gun fire. The vocalist is angry but not overly aggressive, delivering songs with power and emotion. Some of the song titles make me think twice. Stuff like "Little People Eaten by the Moon" and "Power to the Powerful" might sound innocuous enough in a metal arena, but they ring of hubris given what I know. Or what I think I know.

That's the thing about narcissists and people with power. They simply can't help flaunting it. Someone like that will always tell you what they're going to do, because they have to boast. They might try to make it sound like a joke, or a passing comment they laugh off, but it's not. And while these guys might indeed be plausible deniability for the real bastards behind the scenes, I wonder if they're not a little more directly involved than I first suspected.

It's a solid gig and I'm thinking despite that, my visit is a bust, but as they announce their final song, I notice a middle-aged guy move over near one side of the stage. He looks bored, almost annoyed to be there. And he's watching the band with a strange intensity. As they start to play, he half-turns to watch the crowd. He thinks he's being subtle, but honestly, he stands out like the balls on a skinny dog. When someone isn't really into a scene, their presence is always obvious. Like the tourists here in polo shirts. That's why undercover cops are always so easy to spot.

The band starts their song and this one is a little different. It starts slow, a kind of hypnotic melody. The singer starts crooning, but the words are a weird language, a little guttural, a little staccato.

"Eli!"

I startle and Michael is in front of me, his face serious.

"What, man?"

"They're searching for you. They nearly found you."

Not looking up too obviously, I peer out from under my cap and sure enough that one guy is scanning the crowd with intense eyes. A woman I didn't notice before is at the other side of the stage, similarly focused.

"Are they seers?" I ask.

Michael nods. "They're kinda washing through the space with their minds. I can't really explain it, but it's not a pleasant sensation."

I feel Graney hunker down over me more tightly, Sly and Dwight are pressed up close to either side, and Michael is leaning over the table, like he's shielding me. I can see him and see through him at the same time, and those two assholes are looking hard. The crowd is swaying, mesmerized by the weird music.

"They must have anticipated you learning their name," Michael says. "They know you're here."

"No," I say. "They suspect I might be here. They can't know. I expect they're searching all kinds of places. But they won't find me. And now I have someone to follow."

"Risky," Sly says. "Following one of their seers? The people most likely to spot you?"

"Any other choices?"

The ghosts are resounding in their silence.

Simultaneously both goons quit their intense scrutiny of the crowd. The first one I saw subtly nods to the singer, who turns to his band. They give a one, two, three, four, then the drums hammer in and the guitars crunch into a blistering riff.

The crowd surges up out of their apathy, cheering and leaping, headbanging furiously, hands with fingers making horns thrust up into the air. The two who were searching move over to one side, leaning close to talk over the volume of the band. Holy hell, this is a good song. A shame they're connected to whatever these bastards are into, because this band is killer.

As the man and woman talk, hands raised to cup their ears, I see both are wearing a signet ring just like the one I grabbed that started all this. Why didn't I think of that before? A quick glance at the band and I see the singer has one too. Not the rest of the band, as far as I can tell. Interesting. So much for the connection being management.

The two seers frown at the noisy, crowded space and the woman gestures sideways with her head. They move toward the doorway. I want to follow, but they might spot me. I'm guessing they know what I look like, so if I get too close they might see through my dime-store disguise.

"Sit tight," Michael says. "I can't go far, but I'll tail them."

He walks away, dropping into pace behind the pair. Sly and Dwight stay pressed up close beside me. With Graney on my back I feel like I'm in a sludgy, cold puddle.

"Ain't no fucking picnic for us either," Graney growls over my shoulder.

"Too bad you have to shut the fuck up and keep me alive, isn't it."

Sly looks up toward the door, then turns to me. "They're talking. Michael is listening, and I can hear him."

"Okay. What does—"

"Shut the fuck up, man! The woman is saying, *'He's definitely not here, no way someone could hide from both of us.'* The man says, *'So what do we do?'* She says, *'What can we do? Go home, wait for the full, then proceed as normal.'* The dude again, *'And if no one has tracked this prick down by then?'* Michael tells me the woman shrugged, looked uncomfortable, then an awkward silence. Then the guy says, *'Maybe he really did leave. He took his woman to the airport, maybe he slipped away after that.'* And she replies, *'Well, she certainly did. It sticks in my craw that maybe we really lost him. Never lost anyone before.'* He says, *'Only temporary. We'll find them both eventually. For now, we need to concentrate on the full. I'll call you.'* Then Michael says they kinda tapped their signet rings together by way of a handshake or some shit. Says he saw a ripple through the ether when the rings touched, felt a wave of power. Now they're getting into separate cars."

"Follow one!"

Sly glances at me, then concentrates again. "Follow one. I dunno, dude, fucking eeny meeny miny mo."

"What did they mean by 'the full'?" I wonder aloud.

There's a sigh in my right ear and Graney says, "The moon, dickweed. The full moon is the night after tomorrow."

"That's relevant?"

"Jesus fuck," Graney spits. "Weren't you listening to that Luxana chick? She said, and I quote, 'they claim to serve a moon god who is in turn a gateway to cosmic powers beyond the ken of mortal beings like us lowly humans. They are the acolytes of that force here.' So I would think it stands to reason that the full moon is pretty special to them right? Like a monthly sabbath or some shit."

"Good memory," I say.

"It's a cop's ear for detail and retention of pertinent information. You should try it sometime."

"Sure. Or I could just rely on you." Over his grunt of annoyance, I say, "But this is interesting. If they're pissed they can't find me but they need to concentrate on the full moon, it gives us two useful pieces of information."

"Which are?" Dwight says. He looks at the others, his face annoyed. "What?"

"Just felt like you had to get involved, huh?" Sly asks.

Graney chuckles from behind me. "Hush, racist, the grown-ups are talking."

"Fuck all a' y'all!"

"Which are," I say, to stop an argument breaking out. I need these guys close and together to keep me covered. "One, the group is going to be preoccupied with whatever they have to do on the full moon. And two, perhaps the night after tomorrow, they're all going to be in one place for whatever it is they have to do."

"Two days to figure it out and plan an attack?" Sly asks.

"Exactly so."

The Acolytes of Ur finish their set to rapturous applause and cheers. They bow and slap hands with people down the front. The lead singer is distracted, looking out over the crowd with a frown.

"Is he a seer?" I ask Sly, nodding at the young man. He looks like any rock star, denim and a black T-shirt, long brown hair, cheekbones sawing through his thin face like shark's fins.

Sly looks at him for a time, then shakes his head. "Don't think so. Doesn't look the same to me. I can see the aura around his ring, like the others had. But he seems regular otherwise."

I realize Michael is standing in front of me again, looking contrite. I raise an eyebrow at him. "Followed for a few hundred yards, then got wrenched back here," he says. "I think we can't stray too far from you, unless it's to go somewhere you've spent a lot of time. Even then, like while I was checking the apartment, I had to strain against the compulsion to come back. Felt like I was overstretching a big rubber band. I got the plates of both cars, though. Might be useful?"

"Might be. Meanwhile, we concentrate on him." I nod at the lead singer, now helping his band pack up their gear.

The PA is blaring again, playing Korn this time. People are still drinking and partying, though the crowd has thinned a little now the live music is over.

"Concentrate on him?" Michael asks.

"Yeah. I think it's time I met a rock star."

FOURTEEN

I T'S DEFINITELY SAFER to follow someone who isn't able to spot my fucking aura or whatever it is those seers do, but following anyone, singling them out, is not easy. I need him alone, not with the rest of his band. They spend a while packing up and I get the ghosts to watch what happens after they leave the stage. There's a green room out the back and they go there, towel off, crack a few beers, congratulate each other on a kickass gig. I can't disagree with that, they have the chops for sure.

I order another beer while Michael watches the band, reporting back through Sly like before. Nice little arrangement I've got here, able to spy on people as long as they aren't more than a couple of hundred yards away. Better than the damn CIA.

"Michael says they're wheeling their gear out to a van," Sly says. "Bit of a groupie crowd around them, asking for selfies and autographs, but they're slowly getting organized."

I need a vehicle. "Time to go," I say, and slip out the front door.

I flick a glance at the van, parked around the side of the venue near the back. A gaggle of fans is there, obscuring the band members as they load out, but I don't have long.

"If you're going to boost something, do it quietly," Graney says.

"Yeah, yeah. Thanks for the concern, Dad."

He grunts a laugh. But he has a point.

There are cameras all over the place, perched on the corners of buildings like gargoyles. I can't easily boost anything around here without being noticed. A car glides to a stop at the curb of the highway and I see the little white Uber sticker in the back. Someone gets out waving to others near the club, as I jog over.

"Hey buddy, I don't have the app, but you wanna make a hundred bucks cash?"

The young man driving raises an eyebrow. "Maybe."

I respect his caution. "Okay, so I don't want to go into details but I need you to follow that van." I point at the band's black vehicle as it heads for the exit of the parking lot a hundred yards ahead of us. Thankfully it's plain, no bright decals declaring who they are. I guess I respect that caution too.

"What is this, you think you're in a cop movie? Wait, are you a cop?"

"I look like a fucking cop? Seriously, I just need to know where they go. I'm a private eye, but my car got beat up and I can't afford to lose this lead."

"What happens when they get to wherever they're going?"

"I give you a hundred bucks and you fuck off."

I climb in the car to press my case and he shrugs. "Okay, but if they go beyond the suburbs, or it takes more than half an hour, it's another hundred."

"I'll give you a hundred for every half hour it takes. Just keep a few cars between us and them."

He laughs. "I know how to tail someone, man."

"Yeah? Seen a few cop movies? Just be cautious."

My ghosts are lined up in the back seat, watching intently. I still can't get used to seeing only four of them, Alvin Crake conspicuous by his absence.

"We don't really miss him," Michael says with a half-smile. "Guy was kind of an asshole."

I don't bother suggesting that they're all assholes. I guess they already know.

The tail only takes twenty minutes or so. I can tell my driver is disappointed. I pay him and get out about a hundred yards from the apartment complex the band piled into. They locked up the van without unloading, but parked it in a marked space beside the building, so I'm guessing maybe they share a place here. There's four of them, so I hope it's a big apartment. Unless they're two couples or something.

"Now what?" Graney says, voice rasping too close to my ear. "You going in, guns blazing?"

"Not yet."

"Hey, how long have I been here?"

I smile, it's been hours. "Yeah, time to switch out boys."

Dwight moans and bitches as he swaps with Graney, the oily cold making me shudder as they slide over each other and me. I think they're fucking with him, I'm sure Dwight has been given the job twice as much as the others. As I realize, so does he and everyone laughs. Except Dwight who bitches some more.

"All of you shut the fuck up," I say quietly. "Hopefully won't be for much longer. Suck it up."

The apartments all have big balconies and the band appears on one about halfway up, laughing and drinking beers. I hunker in some shadows to watch. At least now I know which is their place, but I still don't want to go in too gung ho. Then I get a lucky break.

Michael appears on the balcony, listening in, reporting back through Sly. Within a minute or two he says, "The singer's name is Bartok, he's leaving. Doesn't live here. The other three do. Seems like he's the boss of the band and they're happy to do what he says. They have another gig tomorrow, but Bartok is heading home."

Sweet.

Moments later I'm tailing Bartok along the sidewalk. It's late, and even though this is the kind of city that never sleeps, these suburban outskirts are a lot quieter. All wide streets and sandy edges and palm trees. The night is mild and dark outside the pools of orange light under the streetlamps.

I guess Bartok here doesn't live far away, as he strolls along the sidewalk, relaxed arms swinging. More fool him. I wait for a dim patch between lights, then run softly up behind him. He hears me at the last moment, turns, a look of mild shock on his face, but all too late. I shoot out a straight right, deliberately oblique, catching him a glancing blow behind the ear. He staggers and goes to one knee, crying out, but his voice is muffled by the dizziness he's suddenly feeling. I grab him and drag him into the shadows, one hand pressed hard across his mouth. I sling him onto his back on the sandy ground, one hand pressed on his face, one holding his arm hard against the sand, my knee pressed into his hip. I'm taller and significantly heavier than he is, and have him pinned like a bug.

"Stay quiet and don't struggle and you get out of this alive."

I honestly don't know right now if that's a lie or not, but I need him to comply.

His eyes are wide and bright in the darkness, but he nods vigorously against my hand. I slowly lift it away. "You yell out, you die."

"We're cool, man." His voice is rushed but muted, his breath fast and shallow. "We're all cool. I have money, you want money? Or what? You want something else? I can get you weed, coke, hey fucking hookers, what do you—"

"I want you to shut the fuck up."

He clams, lips pressed together.

"Take him up on the hookers, cocheese!"

"And the coke, too," Sly says. "When you take shit, we feel it. That's why we like it when you drink."

I roll my eyes at these fools, but don't dignify their nonsense with a response.

"Now, your name is Bartok and you're the lead singer for Acolytes of Ur," I say.

He smiles. "You recognized me, huh?"

Jesus, the hubris of fucking celebrities. "You're also connected to the Acolytes of Ur that aren't band members but a bunch of moon-worshipping fuckwits."

His face drains pale as the moon he bows to and his eyes go wide again. "Oh no, man, don't go there. You need to divert from this path right now, or you die."

"That so."

His wide eyes narrow. "Hey, you're him! The one who took a beacon. They were looking for you at our gig tonight."

Well, I guess the poor bastard doesn't survive this encounter after all. That unfortunate realization was his death warrant.

"Yep, can't leave any loose ends," Graney says.

Typical cop methodology there, but in this case he's right. Damn it, they're a good band.

"Too late for all that, Bartok. I need information."

"Nah nah nah, I can't. They'll kill me. Worse than that, they'll pass me through."

Interesting turn of phrase. "I know the full is the night after tomorrow, Bartok. Where's the meeting?"

"M-m-meeting?"

"You guys have a ritual every full moon, right?"

"How do you know all this stuff? Who the fuck *are* you?"

"I'm justice."

Graney barks a phlegmy laugh right beside me.

"You think you're fucking Batman now?" Sly says, guffawing.

"From ronin to superhero!" Michael says, laughing. Wow, even the one ghost who's supposedly still my friend is ragging on me.

Bartok is struggling against where I'm still holding him down and I realize it's his hand with the ring on it. Something tells me I can't risk that hand getting free. I sit more across his hips, lean hard into his wrist. He stops, eyes narrowing again.

"What do you want?" he asks again.

"Information. Just where to find these fuckers, that's all."

"And what do you plan to do when you get there?"

Suddenly he's all confidence. I don't like that.

"He has a point," Michael says.

"Yeah," Sly agrees. "I mean, say you find out where this moon meeting is, then what? You just storm it, guns blazing?"

I shrug. Honestly, that is pretty much it. It seems to work for me.

"Jesus fuck!" Graney snaps and strides away.

Bartok sighs and I see something shift in his demeanor. "I might as well tell you. I mean, it'll do you no good and I'm already done for. You're not going to let me go, are you? Because you know I'll tell them this happened. Even if I promise not to, you won't believe me."

"That doesn't mean you have to die," I tell him. "You guys are a killer band. Maybe you can just keep doing that. I will have to have you detained for a while. Tell me what I want to know and I'll lock you up safe and secure somewhere until after the full."

"But you won't survive the full, so who will ever let me out."

"How about I schedule a message to go to someone, one of your bandmates maybe? For the day after. If I don't survive the message still gets outs."

There's a part of me that wants to make this work. I've killed so many motherfuckers, it's just part of the job, but that doesn't mean I'm a mindless murderer. If I can avoid killing, that's good. I have no qualms about killing actual bad guys. All the fuckers who I've ended pretty much deserved it one way or another. But this kid feels different. Perhaps he's not deep into this cult yet and maybe he can survive. He can't be much over twenty years old. I don't want to be the bad guy all the time. Sometimes there's a choice.

It makes me think of old mythology. I've never liked the trope that vampires have to be invited in, for example. That's some "free will" religious bullshit that blames the victim. Anyone with half a brain knows damn well that evil just happens to people, no invite required. But we can try to exercise free will to avoid evil, to fight against it. If I can fuck up these Acolyte weirdoes without taking this kid down, I'll do it. Give him a second chance. I can find a storage unit or something, tie him up there. He'll have a miserable couple of days, then be let out. Either by me, or his friends. I can try to do the right thing, can't I?

"Going fucking soft," Graney growls.

"Soft in the damn head, cocheese."

"You mean it?" Bartok asks.

"Yeah. I do."

"Okay." He nods, takes a deep breath. "Yeah, okay." He gives me an address. "Penthouse, right at the top. You get there, you'll see wonders. But you won't get there."

I have to hope he's telling me the truth. As backup, I ask, "What about some names? Give me some high ups in the group."

Bartok laughs, reels off a few names. These are not little people. He's naming internationally known stars and politicians. "Won't do you any good, Batman."

He's fucking laughing at me now. "Come on then."

I move my knee, trying to think of where I might lock this guy up. Maybe a motel room with a Do Not Disturb sign on the door will do it for a couple of days if I tie and silence him well enough.

I'm wary, watching him as he stands, waiting to see if he'll bolt or fight, maybe go for a weapon. But he just brushes himself off. He looks up, eyes kind of sad. "You won't survive it," he says. He raises his hand to his head. The one with the signet ring on it.

He presses the ring against his temple and all my ghosts cry out, "No!" at the same moment as Bartok mutters something.

My ghosts reel and stagger back as if hit with a shockwave and Bartok's eyes roll up to show the whites. Blood runs from his ears and nostrils and he drops, dead.

"Get the fuck out of here," Michael says urgently. "That was like a fucking alarm bell ringing out for miles. They'll know exactly where this just happened."

But I'm already running.

FIFTEEN

"**W**HY DO YOU CARE, MAN?" Sly asks from my back. It's too weird when they talk to me so close-up. And that cold, oily sensation won't go away.

Michael gestures at him, as if to say, *Well?*

I guess they have a point. Why do I care?

"Gonna get yourself good and dead," Graney says.

"You ain't fucking Batman, cocheese. What's the point?"

"Just leave," Michael says, but I hear a kind of resignation in his voice. He knows I won't quit. "Get outta town, wait for Bridget to call, meet her in fucking Macau or Manila or something."

I pace back and forth in the motel room on the edge of Seven Hills. I figure it's far enough out of town to be safe for now. I rented a small car with one of my fake IDs to get here. I'm glad I always keep that stuff with me, not left in the ransacked apartment. In recent months I've got in the habit of wearing one of those traveler's belts that goes on under your shirt. Call me paranoid, I don't care. I'm used to the slightly bulky discomfort of it, but it means I always have my alternate IDs, a chunk of cold, hard cash, and a few other bits with me. Means I can lay low like this without risking exposure.

I wish I could go back to the apartment, try to salvage some clothes and other stuff, but I can't risk it. I have the clothes on my back, my phone and wallet, and my two CZ 75s, that's it. I guess I need to go shopping.

"They'll find us," I say eventually, even as I'm wondering if that's true. But I think it is. "Either I hit them on my terms, or I'm constantly watching over my shoulder, running defense. The best defense is offense, remember?" I do actually believe that. It makes perfect sense. Only a fuckwit would wait for someone to hit them before fighting back. If you know someone means to hurt you, fucking destroy them instantly with extreme prejudice. You may never survive the first strike otherwise.

"You really think they give a shit about you?" Graney asks.

"I don't know for sure, but I hurt a bunch of their guys. And now the singer from that band. That really sucks, the band was good."

"They'll love that," Sly says in my ear. "The Acolytes of Ur—the band, I mean—suddenly have a whole lot of attention. The lead singer dead, they get loads of press, the evil group get to hide further behind the public profile of the band. Then the band audition for a new singer, they're back on stage in six months. Maybe less. You probably did them a favor, they can't buy publicity like that."

It's a grim assessment but he makes a kind of sense. Regardless, I still don't believe this group will let me get away with it, even if that aspect does work for them rather than against.

I'm about to say something else when I realize the ghosts are looking at each other with frowns. Dwight starts to speak then

Michael, Sly and Graney all simultaneously tell him to shut up. Michael tips his head to one side, like he's listening.

A trickle of ice finds its way into my gut. Have they tracked us down again? Am I wearing ghosts like fucking backpacks for no reason?

"How did you find us?" Michael asks.

Shit.

"Oh, I suppose that makes sense," Michael says.

"What the fuck is happening?" I demand through gritted teeth.

"It's Luxana," Graney tells me, while Michael concentrates. "She found you because she could look for us. She's seen us, after all."

"She says the way of hiding from the Acolytes still works," Michael tells me, gesturing at Sly on my back.

"Enough of this," Michael's voice is suddenly strangely high. His entire expression changes, almost like he's morphing into someone else. Graney and Dwight stagger away from him, Sly on my back curses. "I'll talk to you directly."

I'm looking at Michael but hearing Luxana, I know that without a doubt. "Good to hear from you, I guess. Unless it's bad news?"

"Frankly, I'm amazed you're still alive. Well done."

"You told me how to hide from them."

"Well, yes, I theorized a possible method. I'm glad it worked."

"You didn't know?"

"Not for certain. This isn't an everyday situation, Eli."

I suppose I can't argue with that. "So why are you here?"

"I've been doing a bit of research and, as you are still alive and still in Las Vegas, I thought I'd share what I've learned."

"Tell him to leave!" Graney says.

"Yeah, lady!" Dwight says. "Tell this dickhole to get the fuck out."

Michael turns to face them but it's clearly Luxana who says, "Hush." They're a little offended and I can't help but laugh at that. Fucking children. She looks back to me. "These are bad and powerful people, Eli. You sure you want to tangle with them?"

"I don't think I have a choice. They'll hunt me, right?"

"I don't know. But it is a strong possibility."

"So I take it to them. That's my style."

Luxana sighs. "Okay then. Well, know this. They meet every month on the full moon, to do their twisted thing."

"Yeah, I learned that recently. And I know where the next meeting is, in two days."

Luxana raises Michael's eyebrows in surprise. "You have been busy. Your timing is good too, because this full moon is a special one. There are a whole bunch of things the moon gets saddled with, all the old monthly names like Wolf Moon, Buck Moon, Harvest Moon, Hunter's Moon, you know about those, right?"

"I've heard of them…"

"Okay, doesn't really matter. Mostly they're just in reference to the time of year. Hunter's Moon is the one in October because that's when the deer are fat from a whole summer of good eating, so it's the best time to hunt. In the northern hemisphere anyway. But there are other moons that are infrequent and therefore more powerful. A Blood Moon, for example."

"I know that one. Full lunar eclipse, right? When the Earth gets between the moon and the sun, so the only light the moon gets is from around the edges of the Earth and it looks red."

"Clever boy. Air molecules from Earth's atmosphere scatter out the majority of the blue light, so what's left reflects onto the Moon with a red glow. Now tell me what a Blue Moon is."

I have to stop and think about that, but I know I've read about it before.

"Two full moons in the same calendar month," Sly says from over my shoulder.

Michael's eyes flick up to him and back to me with a smile in them. She makes him look so different, it's freaky. "That's the common thought, but not actually correct. Each year, the moon finishes its last cycle about eleven days before Earth finishes its orbit around the sun, so there's an offset. Those days add up and there's an extra full moon every two and a half years or so. That's the original definition of a Blue Moon, the third full moon of a season containing four full moons instead of three."

"Okay, so what?" I say.

"So, imagine if a Blue Moon and a Blood Moon coincided," Michael-Luxana says.

"A Blueblood Moon," Graney says with a grin. "It's a fucking British monarch?"

Michael's glance of derision silences him and Luxana's gaze falls back on me. "This is a significant astronomical event, Eli. And the Acolytes of Ur lap that stuff up. The meeting this time isn't just the local chapter, but acolytes from around the country, even around the world, are going to be there. You hit them now, you'll hit about every major player in their sick cabal."

"Well, isn't that a nice coincidence."

"Is it?" Luxana's eyes are serious in Michael's face. "Or is it why you're here? Are you the agent of something else, you and these spirits? Are you here because some powerful destiny wills it?"

I don't like the sound of that at all. I hate all the preordained destiny and fate bullshit. I'm with Sarah Connor, there is no fate but that which we make for ourselves. Also, and once again, so what? Does it matter why I'm here now? I am here, and I'm planning some mayhem. Let that be enough.

"Whatever," I say aloud. "Bad luck for those fuckers. A roomful of pedophiles, corrupt politicians, immoral business leaders, whatever else you said before? Sounds like my kind of shooting gallery."

Luxana's smile softens Michael's face. It's sad. "I don't think you'll even get close. But imagine if you did!"

"You didn't think I'd last this long, but here I am."

"Fair point. These people, Eli, they control through fear. Everything is driven by fear. Everyone is afraid of something. Find out what, and you control them. These are the kind of people who exploit that relentlessly, in media, in politics, in everyday life. And they enhance their power and influence enormously through the energy they absorb via some entity through the moon. They are not playing on a level field. The energy they exploit radiates off this entity, some intelligence, that exists so far outside our understanding we couldn't comprehend it if we tried. I'm not sure of their rituals, but the rituals are designed to expose them to that... radiation, for want of a better term. Honestly, I don't know if you even *can* fight something like that."

"Everyone has a weakness. Why would this godlike thing give these scumbags anything anyway?"

"I imagine it has no idea. Their ritual simply opens a portal, focused through a full moon. They get the power by taking it without permission. If the entity knew, who knows what might happen? But how would it even notice? Like rain washing the dirt from a road, the cloud above isn't aware of the cleaning taking place. We are insignificant. The cosmos cares not for the dust."

"There truly is no resource the rich won't exploit," Sly says.

He's not wrong.

"Well, thank you, Luxana. I appreciate the information."

"If you are going against these bastards, I hope you succeed. I doubt you will, but good luck."

I nod, and then Michael blinks and his face shifts, his eyes darken. "Fuck that," he mutters.

"What did she feel like *inside* you?"

"Shut the fuck up, Dwight!" we all say at once.

SIXTEEN

GOD BLESS AMERICA, the guns and ammo shop half a block from my motel is more than happy to stock me up against one of my fake IDs. Once I've got my gear, I'm planning to lay low a little longer, do some planning. I pick up two more CZ 75s and a shit-ton of ammo for them, in multiple spare clips. One of those lame-ass hunting jackets with all the pockets comes in useful. They even have it in black. I pick up two bowie knives and calf sheaths for those. A couple of mace sprays, the high velocity, extra spicy kind. Then I grab a good pump-action shotgun, a Benelli Nova in anodized matte black. Twelve gauge and 4+1 rounds, I make sure to get a couple of extra boxes of shells too. I may or may not have reload time, but best to be prepared.

I learned the joys of the shotgun off Vernon Sykes. He was the kind of sick bastard who would never kneecap a guy with a pistol if he could blow off a foot with a shotgun. He always said the Benelli Nova was the most reliable one out there. I've never had reason to doubt that assessment, even if I am glad Vernon is dead now.

The shotgun is good for close-up and wildfire work. Once I'm in, my marksmanship skills with handguns will be all I need. I hope.

"Jesus, buddy, planning a party, huh?" the shopkeeper says once it's all on the counter.

"This'll show up on a police scanner somewhere," Graney says from my back. "Or maybe this guy is a conscientious shop owner and will directly report you himself."

I don't give a shit. In a little over twenty-four hours I'll be in the thick of it, then I'll be dead or gone. They won't find me in that short time, not with the ID I'm using.

"It looks like a lot," I say aloud. "My house got broken into and robbed. They took our home defense stuff." I gesture at the CZ 75s and the shotgun. "I'm just replacing it. Lucky I wasn't home, or they'd have had firsthand experience with the ones they stole before they got close."

The gun seller grunts a laugh. "I hear that. Chickenshit thieves only ever slink around in the dark."

I lock the weaponry in the trunk of the rented car, then head over to a clothing store. I get a few sets of new clothes so I can finally change, and a long coat. I'll need to conceal the shotgun on my way in. I also buy a new sports bag for my clothes, and I can jury-rig the shoulder strap of that to hold the shotgun in a kind of cross-body harness. It'll hang inside the coat, leaving my hands free, but can be easily grabbed and swung into a firing position. After that, it's food and snacks, then I'm ready to camp and wait for tomorrow night.

Back in the motel room I'm getting all the gear organized when a text message comes through. I smile, expecting Bridget. She's the only one who knows this phone, we have one each just for ourselves. I already dumped my other one once I knew this cabal were after me. Like I said, call me paranoid if you like. It's not paranoia when they really are out to get you.

But it's not Bridget. It's a list of names, lots of people I recognize, including a couple of ex-presidents, some major Hollywood types, a handful of world-famous billionaires. At the end it says,

Thought you might like to have an idea who you're up against. Lux x

"How the fuck did she get this number?" I say.

"I gave it to her," Michael says. "She asked me."

"How do you know it?"

He gives me a look and I have to ignore that. The mind-reading, the shared thoughts, I can't tell where they start and finish, how much these fuckers know.

"I pay more attention than the other three," Michael says, maybe trying to make me feel better.

I like the way they're actively helping me now, but I'm not so keen on them freely communicating with the world at large. There are seismic shifts happening in my life, and I don't like that.

"High profile list," Graney says. "That won't go unnoticed if you wipe out any of these folks."

"Especially if you wipe out all of them," Sly says.

"He won't get past the front damn door," Dwight says.

"I'll be doing the world a favor. It'll be a better place without all these pricks."

"Even the billionaire entrepreneurs, cocheese? You resent their success that much?"

"Especially those fuckers! Being a billionaire is not a success, it's a massive moral failure."

"A *moral* failure?"

"Of course. No billionaire is made without colossal exploitation, then they sit on their fortune like a dragon on a hoard of gold, just keeping it for no reason at all. No fucker *needs* a billion dollars. To be a billionaire while people around the world starve and die of preventable sickness is an atrocity. To have the means to end poverty and choose not to? That's about the biggest fucking failure possible. Successful entrepreneurs, my ass."

"That is actually a fair point," Graney says with a laugh.

"No rich person—like, really hundreds of millions or more rich—ever got there without other people suffering for them. Even the brats who inherit the money, they're inheriting blood-stained riches. Fuck 'em all."

"You trying to rationalize your choice here, man?" Sly asks.

"What do you mean?"

"You could leave it all behind. I know you keep saying they'll hunt you down, but you're hiding now. Keep hiding, you don't have to die for these assholes."

"He's right," Michael says. "We'll keep you hidden, the heat will ease, we can start again elsewhere."

I smirk at them. "You're protecting your own asses. I have a mission here. Ever since the thing with Carly I've been atoning for my past. It's led me to this. I don't truck with all the fate bullshit, but there is cause and effect. Whatever occurred before has led me here and I plan to see it through. If I pull this off, I'm doing a massive service to all of humanity. Look at that list! I wipe all those fuckers out, just think of the knock-on effect. I'll take them down or die trying. Maybe that *is* why I've survived until now. Maybe it is fate. Who cares? It's a job worth doing and I plan to do it. You lot want to stick around longer, then fucking help me."

"Holy sheee-it," Dwight says. "You really think you are Batman. Gonna get us all kilt."

SEVENTEEN

PATIENCE IS A VIRTUE in any walk of life, but especially the violent life. It seems like a contradiction, everyone thinks violence is fast and furious. It often is in final execution, but that's the end point. More people die and suffer from rushing in than anything else in fighting. There's an old adage I learned from a kung fu teacher, Sifu Richard, I trained with many years ago. I spent a lot of time studying all kinds of fighting systems, not just gunplay. I'm an all-rounder when it comes to fucking people up. Anyway, this guy, he was a real traditionalist and a real badass. Took that old-fashioned stuff and trained it properly, knew how to make it work like it was supposed to.

"So many people these days don't get it," I remember him saying, anger in his eyes. "And it gives the traditional arts a bad name. People reduce the knowledge to a bunch of flashy moves they don't understand and then they propagate bullshit. But the old arts are genuinely deadly when you understand the applications, and the proper way to train them. They used this shit on battlefields, for fuck's sake, and they killed motherfuckers. Just because assholes these days don't understand it, doesn't mean the arts are no good."

I liked Sifu Richard a lot, we got along well.

Anyway, the old adage. I don't remember the Chinese terminology, but I really internalized the principle. Sifu Richard would always talk about the four tenets of good fighting: patience, focus, accuracy, and passion.

The idea is that you wait patiently in the first instance. Don't rush in, take your time, assess a situation, feel an opponent out as much as you're able. But never lose focus. Then when the opportunity comes, be accurate, exploit the opening with dead-eyed precision, and with passion. With absolute, relentless intent. Patience, focus, accuracy, passion. I've always remembered that and it's never let me down. In the times when I've fucked up, it's usually because I let one of those key principles slide.

So, sitting back in the motel room waiting for the moment to strike was easy. That was the patience. The focus was easy too, I didn't let myself get distracted. I didn't do something else while I waited. I ordered in food, I trained as much as the space allowed, I kept my weapons in top condition. The patience and focus were there. The accuracy comes next, and that's easy too. I know exactly where I'm going. I went out once and did a couple of drive-bys to check the building. I can't know more about it until I get there. But that's the chaos. No matter how much you plan, in the end fighting is always responding to chaos. You never know for sure what your opponent is going to do. But that's okay. That's the fun of it all.

In terms of accuracy, I also got a bit more information from Luxana. I sent her a text.

As you have my number, want to let me know the exact moment of the full?

She replied back not long after.

10:47 p.m. Penumbral Eclipse begins
11:44 p.m. Partial Eclipse begins
1:11 a.m. Total Eclipse begins (completely red moon)
1:18 a.m. Maximum Eclipse (Moon is closest to the center of the shadow)
1:25 a.m. Total Eclipse ends
2:52 a.m. Partial Eclipse ends
3:49 a.m. Penumbral Eclipse ends
So if they draw power from the height of the astronomical event, they'll be focusing on 1:18 a.m. You get there after 1:25 a.m. and you'll probably have missed it.
Good luck!

That was a hell of a lot more information that I expected, or maybe even needed. But when it comes to accuracy, that covers it. I figure these assholes will be busiest about 1:00 a.m. onwards.

Patience, focus, accuracy, and passion. Thank you, Sifu Richard.

I've been patient, and focused. Accuracy has me walking up to the building in question at exactly 1:00 a.m. Now comes the fourth tenet of fighting. Passion. Absolute intent.

Let's rock'n'roll.

The moon is full and massive, right above us, already almost entirely obscured by the shadow of the Earth. The curved shadow on the moon surface feels heavy to look at. I lose sight of it as I get close to the building, a tower of condos, glass and cement with a slight wave shape to the design. I need the penthouse right at the top. The first challenge is getting in the front doors, but we have a plan for that. As I walk up there's a concierge desk opposite the double glass entry and a security guard looks up. I wondered if there might be a bigger presence here, but I guess they don't expect me to come right to them. More hubris on their part. Then again, maybe this is suicide. We'll see.

The guard raises an eyebrow at the guy all in black wearing a long coat, standing calmly outside. I have a cap pulled low, a hood over it, thin gloves to mask my prints. What the guard doesn't see while he's taking me in is Michael, right there in the lobby, blood dripping from the craterous wound in the side of his head as he goes to the door and presses the button to exit. These buildings are designed to stop anyone without a pass or keycard getting in, but getting out is easy. One button, usually big and green. Michael's face twists in a grimace of pain, then the glass doors separate with a hiss and I stride in.

The security guard's laconically raised eyebrow is joined by its twin in a shocked look of surprise and he starts to stand up. I can't let him get the jump on me, but this guy is pretty innocent, so I try to go easy.

"Hold it, buddy," he says, raising a palm to me. His other hand is moving toward his hip.

I swing up the Benelli from under my coat and shake my head.

He freezes, frowns at the door. "How did you?"

Then I've rounded the desk even as he tries to scurry back, but I'm too fast, my fist whipping out across the point of his jaw. He grunts and drops like a sack of butter. I duck with him, shooting a hand under his head to stop him cracking his skull open on the glossy marble floor, then switch my grip to his collar and drag him behind me. We go around to the elevators and there's a door marked EMERGENCY EXIT. That'll be the stairs.

As he starts to moan and writhe gently, about to wake up, I pat him down and find the holy grail—his passkey. One of those electronic ones like a thick credit card. I don't know how far it'll get me, but it will hopefully at least let me operate the elevator and save me running up thirty-six flights of stairs.

I blip the stairwell door open then pocket the keycard and drag the poor fool through. He's starting to protest and struggle, but still hasn't got his wherewithal back and I bring out the zip ties, secure him easily, hands and feet, through the railings at the foot of the stairs. I rip out the front of his shirt, twist it into a gag, and tie that to muffle any screaming for help he might try.

"The fuck, man?" he manages, just before I wedge it in place.

"Sorry, pal. Just sit tight and be patient, yeah? This is all finished for you now if you mind your business. Someone will find you, in the morning at the latest." I pat his shoulder. "Be good, okay?"

Then I'm back in the lobby pressing the button for the elevator. When I go in, I press for the top floor, but even though the security guard's pass card made the green light on the panel light up, the button for the top floor won't operate. Frowning, I try the next floor down. That one works.

"Looks like even security doesn't get to the top," Graney says. "What makes you think you can?"

"I'll try the stairs."

It feels entirely surreal to be standing in an elevator, armed to the teeth, slowly ascending while soft Muzak plays. My ghosts are crammed in with me, all looking apprehensive.

"Think this is the end?" I ask.

Sly shakes his head, looks away. I can see the panel of elevator buttons through the gaping hole in his torso, bits of rib poking through here and there like broken teeth.

"Probably is the end," Graney growls, throat raw, wet, dripping red.

"You're a fucking fool, cocheese. Gonna die for these assholes." I can't see Dwight perched on my back, but I know his bullet hole, right between the eyes, always trickles rivulets of scarlet down his nose and into his stubbly cheeks.

"You can still turn around," Michael says. "This is your last chance."

I watch the blood drip from the atrocious exit wound from my bullet, spatter on his shoulder. All their blood, all their corrupted bodies, they focus me in a way. I can picture wounds like these appearing on my enemies up there, delivered with extreme prejudice.

"You know I'm not gonna quit," I say.

"Probably get stuck one floor too low anyway," Graney says. "That'd be pretty fucking funny."

The elevator pings, the doors slide open. I already have the shotgun up and leveled at the lobby outside, but it's empty of people. Nice dark blue carpeting, green plants in terracotta pots against the far wall. The lobby leads left and right to a few condos, the door to the stairway and emergency exit are opposite. I stride quickly across, tap the pass card and the panel above the door handle turns green. I step into the cool, cement-smelling stairs, fluorescent lights harsh after the soft orange glow in the hallway.

As the door clicks behind me, Michael says, "Last chance, Eli." But I ignore him and start up, shotgun at the ready.

"The penthouse is two levels," Sly says.

"What?"

"We came out here and counted, remember? Thirty-six stories.

The top button on the elevator was thirty-five, but you had to get out on thirty-four. So now we're going up to thirty-five. Means the penthouse has two levels."

I pause for a moment, wondering if that matters. Whatever they're doing up there, will it be on the upper floor? Maybe they even have an exit to the roof and a veranda or something. I guess I'll have to assume that is the case and go in quietly if I can. I nod at Sly and start up again.

As I reach the door to the penthouse level my ghosts are milling around me nervously. The cold, oily feeling of Dwight Ramsey riding me grows tighter, like he's hugging me for comfort. Man, I won't miss having one of these bastards on my back every second.

"Feels bad," Sly says.

"Yeah, horrible energy up there," Graney says, looking up like he can see through the floor.

I shrug. "I guess that's because they already started. But that's good, I want them busy. I need more help now. Can one of you go through, tell me what's on the other side of that door?"

Michael steps past me, pushes through. A moment later he's back. "The other side is a hallway, a few doors either side, all bedrooms, I think. Elevator at the end. It opens out into a large lounge area. I didn't see farther. There's someone standing right there." He points at the door.

"Standing guard, you mean?"

"I guess so. And there are some people in the lounge farther up, I couldn't see how many. I've never been there before so I could only go a little way from you before I got hauled back."

"Okay then." I reach up and tap lightly on the door, a polite knock.

Nothing happens.

"You're knocking?" Graney asks.

I tap a little harder. A little more insistent, but not too loud. Hopefully only the guy right on the other side will hear. Come on, who can ignore a knock at the door. Especially one where no one is supposed to be.

There's a click and it cracks open halfway, a burly guy with dark hair and a neat, short beard looks out, frowning. "You got the wrong fl—"

He doesn't finish the sentence because one of my razor-honed bowie knives open his throat right back to his spine. I grab him with my free hand and twist my body, hauling him through to send him in a header down the stairs. He smears bright red against the pale cement as he tumbles down, managing a kind of burbling grunt as he rag-dolls, no doubt already dead, or close enough to it. I slip in and quietly close the door behind me, lean against it. The pale cream carpet is plush as hell, which is excellent for stealth. I stare along the hallway, some forty feet or more before it opens out into a living room, but it seems no one heard. No one is coming. I can see the edge of white leather sofas and armchairs, one pair of feet crossed at the ankle as someone sits back in one. Glimpses of glass-topped chrome tables and beyond all that a wall of glass looking out over the Las Vegas night. I hear a TV burbling, a low murmur of conversation. There's more than one guy in there and I need to stay quiet if I can. Seems unlikely though.

I creep along the hallway, looking into each room. There's three one side, two the other, then the elevator. The first two doors are ajar, darkened bedrooms beyond. Second on the left is a bathroom, massive and marble with a huge hot tub. The last door on either side is closed. I move up to the one on left and nod at Michael.

He leans his head through the door, then comes back. "A study or office. Dark, no one there."

I point at the last door on the right, moving a little closer. He looks in. "Big ass bedroom, got a four-fucking-poster bed in there. Lights are on, but no one there."

I slide along the wall until I'm close to the end of the hallway, tip my head at it.

Michael and Sly walk forward, Graney moves a little away from me. Not sure why they're spreading out. "Four guys in here," Michael says. "Stairs on the other side up to another level. Must be where the action is. These four look bored, like they're waiting."

It feels wrong, them just standing there talking in normal conversational tones. I know intellectually that no one else can see them or hear them, but would it hurt them to pretend to be cautious? Maybe whisper at least. Then a thought occurs to me. What if there's someone like Luxana here who *can* see them? I guess I'll find out soon enough.

I move back down the hallway, gesturing my ghosts to follow. I need to split these four up a little if I can, and I don't have much time before the eclipse reaches full. I push open the door to one of the farthest bedrooms, step into the shadows and then call out. "Hey! Little help?"

I hope to hell they don't all come.

"The fuck, Tony?" someone shouts.

Tony's dead, motherfucker. "Help me out here!" I call.

"Jesus fuck," there's more muttering and I hear movement.

My ghosts are in the hall and Sly says, "One guy coming, big, but more fat than muscle. No gun in sight."

"The fuck are you, Tony?"

"In here."

"You sound fucking weird, man, what the hell?"

He goes to the wrong door, the one opposite where I'm hiding. That's okay, I can work with it. I step briskly across the hall, slap a hand across his mouth and keep going, drive him forward into the room. My bowie knife slams in between his ribs, one, two, three times, the deep *chunk* of it muffled by his weight. He flinches and cries out against my palm, but I reach around and stab him again, this time hard in the chest, hugging tight to me. He slackens and I let him slide to the floor, keeping his mouth covered just in case.

He rolls onto his side, eyes wild, blood bubbling out around my palm. I can tell the fight has gone and I step back.

"The fuck?" he whispers, then his eyes glaze.

"What's happening down there?" a voice calls.

Graney is at the bedroom door. "Another one coming, skinny."

"Where are you two? You know how they feel about us going in any of the rooms. Guys?"

"He's pausing," Graney says. "Smarter, this one. He's suspicious. Okay, he's pulled a piece and he's coming slowly."

Oh well, I guess the stealth ends here. Two down, at least, that leaves only three downstairs. I unhook the shotgun, throw the strap away, and take a deep breath. Here we go.

A quick roll has me out of the door in a crouch, much lower down than this mook would expect. Even as his eyes lock on, the shotgun booms and his chest disintegrates as he flies back, spraying the clean, pale walls with blood. As voices burst out, I'm already up and striding, racking another shell. One guy appears at the end of the hall and I blow his head away, then I'm stepping into the main room. The last of the four is running the other way, heading for the far side. I quicken my pace, rack, and fire. He launches forward as his back blooms scarlet, slams into the wall and slides down it into a heap.

The view of the city from up here is epic, glass walls on both sides of the big room. The TV is showing some late-night chat show, a beautiful Hollywood star sharing some anecdote. A quick scan proves no one else is nearby so I keep moving, across the massive space. An entire floor of a building for three bedrooms, an office, and a living room. How the one percent live.

On the far side of the main living space is another small hallway, a room off to one side with linens, washer, dryer, other stuff. Opposite that are stairs going up, floating design with glass siding.

"This energy is bad, man," Sly says.

All the ghosts are wincing now, acting like they're caught in the winds of a powerful storm. I don't have time to care. Feet come hammering down the stairs, so I blow them away at the knee through the glass. Crystalline squares glitter and sparkle as they rain down, spattered red, and the screaming is high and panicked as the man hits the stairs and slides down. I round the end of the stairway, looking up to see another guy in a track suit just appearing at the top, automatic pistol in hand. He starts to swing it toward me, but doesn't have time before I blow him backwards.

Angry shouting erupts upstairs as I drop the shotgun, no time to reload, and draw a brace of CZ 75s. I finish the guy whose knees I took out, then both hands are leveling barrels up the stairs. I start to climb.

"Anyone laying in wait?" I ask.

Michael, Sly, and Graney all look down from the landing above and shake their heads. "Not if you're quick," Michael says.

Seems like maybe all these guys so far were just waiting around for their bosses. The Acolytes really didn't expect me to come for them. I'm almost offended at their lack of concern.

But I hear more voices up there. I run and find myself in wide kind of lobby, neatly carpeted like downstairs, tables against the walls with expensive-looking vases and other ornaments.

In front of me is a short hallway, one door either side, and then dark wood double-doors at the end. I can hear chanting coming from beyond the double doors. My ghosts are grimacing, bracing to stand still, their spectral hair swimming in a static wind I can't feel or hear.

"Look out!" Michael manages through gritted teeth, just as both doors on either side swing open and four men lean out into the hallway. They're all armed and bullets fly.

I'm moving on autopilot. As soon as the doors started to open, I went down and right. As the first face appeared, I put a bullet in it. It disappeared back as another on that side leveled his weapon and fired. Still moving I jerked backwards, my leg and lower back screaming at the sudden change in direction, muscles forcing bones to move in strange angles. The wall right beside my head explodes as the round hits it. That would have gone through my head first if I hadn't managed to shift.

The two from the opposite door start firing, but I hit the deck and roll around the corner of the hallway. I stand up, press my back to the wall, guns ready. Three of them there and at least one a damn good shot. Or maybe he was lucky. I'll err on the side of caution and consider him a marksman.

I dip a shoulder forward, revealing just an inch of myself for a fraction of a second before ducking back, and a hail of bullets tears up the wall. They're crouched and ready, tigers waiting to pounce.

"They're in the hallway," Graney says. "Three abreast, just standing there, weapons leveled."

"You're pinned down," Michael says.

"Now what?" Sly asks.

"Goddammit, cocheese, you fucking had to be Batman."

"Hold tight!" I whisper, then roll, using my shoulder like a break-fall to keep my hands free, right across the mouth of the hallway to the other side. Bullets rain, but as I go, I rapid fire from both CZ 75s, peppering the area as widely as possible.

There are screams of pain, but I'm gritting my teeth against my own hurt. My body was low enough to catch them out, but one of them got a bullet into my leg as I went over, punching into the meat of my right calf about four inches below the back of my knee. Went right through, but it hurts like a motherfucker and it's bleeding hard. Fuck it.

I have to take a chance, I can't let that keep bleeding. I put my guns on the ground, sitting where I rolled, and shrug out of the long coat. I rip out a section of lining, fold it into as thick a bandage as possible and start to bind my leg tight. Not tourniquet-tight, but close to it. I have to be able to move, but I need to stop that bleed. The pain is high and electric, makes me breathe fast and shallow, agony whistling from my leg up just about every nerve ending I have. I try to breathe through it, use the hurt to focus. I am not getting dizzy. I am definitely not getting fucking dizzy.

"At least tell me I got one of 'em," I snarl through gritted teeth.

"Two, actually," Sly says. "One down, curled up around a gut-shot. He's as good as finished. Another you clipped in the shoulder. He's hurt and switched his gun to his other hand."

"Might put off his aim, at least," I say.

"Third one coming around the corner any second though," Graney says urgently.

Fuck! I drag the knot tight and snatch up a pistol just as the guy steps around the wall. The only thing that saves me is his assumption I would have moved farther back. He's looking just over and past me as he rounds the wall, and in the moment it takes his eyes and gun to track a little lower I pump three bullets, championship grouping, right in his chest. He's dead before he hits the ground.

Howling against the hurt through my calf, I stand and step into the hallway entrance, trusting the guy with the gun in his off-hand might be a fraction slower than me. It's all I need. And I get it. We fire simultaneously, but his first shot goes wide. Mine doesn't. He fires twice more, but so do I and mine all find their mark while his find the ceiling.

Double doors at the end of the short hallway are all that stand between me and whatever these bastards are up to. My ghosts stand in front of me, grimacing, their hair whipping around like they're standing in a gale. Which is weird, because it's still and silent except for the moaning of the gutshot mook and my own ragged breath.

I kick the mook hard, right under the chin, and he's out. Let him bleed slow and quiet now.

"What's beyond?" I ask, nodding at the doors, trying to ignore the searing pain in my calf.

They shake their heads.

"Can't tell," Michael says with a wince. He tries to walk forward, but it's like he's glued in place. "Whatever's happening, we can't get close."

"That's inconvenient," I say.

Oh well, nothing for it, I suppose. I hope they're busy in there, enough to give me a moment. I lift my good leg, balancing painfully on the injured one, and drive my foot into the middle of the doors. My guns are held level, one in each hand, ready.

The doors bang back and there's five…no six mooks all lined up, AR15s or something similar trained on me. Four men, two women, all hard-faced as hell. I could start firing, but I'd be mincemeat in seconds.

Well, fuck. I hoped to get farther than this.

"Well done, dick cheese" Graney says. "You killed all the bodyguards, all the little people, and the rich and corrupt are untouched. Again. You're just another cog in their fucking machine."

Why is no one firing? My fingers twitch on the triggers. Could I drop six people with automatics? I'm good, but at about ten feet range? No one's that good.

"I want him alive!" a voice yells. "I'll take my time with him when we're done here."

My gaze, until now entirely occupied with the bristling barrels of my imminent death, moves past the line of armed guards and I see the room beyond. It's large, like a lounge area with more of those white leather sofas and armchairs. A bar along one side, massive TV screen taking up half a side wall. A couple of doors lead off the other side. But the room only takes up half the level. On the far side are glass bifold doors, all slid back so the entire wall is open to a massive rooftop patio. It's easily half the size of the entire floor, a pool at one end with a hard cover over it, lots of tables and chairs and sun loungers all pushed back to the sides. A glass railing wraps around the three sides not connected to the room, offering a massive view out across the city. But it's the naked people that really catch my eye.

There must be thirty or forty of them, various ages, men and women. Some are instantly recognizable, powerful politicians, ex-presidents, movie stars, TV anchors, business leaders. Others I have no idea who they are, but they seem equally at home in the crowd.

One man, easily late 60s, fat and balding, his penis almost lost in a thick tuft of gray pubic hair, points into the corner of the room near the bar. "Tie him up good." Then he turns back to the group. They're moving into a rough circle, taking up the vast majority of the huge patio, chanting, looking up. This whole venture, me making it this far, has taken less than fifteen minutes. A big digital clock on the wall reads 1:16 a.m. Two minutes until the full eclipse.

The armed guards move forward. The two women step aside to cover me while the men grab me and drag me into the room. Kinda sexist. The red moon, the Blood Moon which is also a Blue Moon, is massive and directly above the gathering circle outside. The guards strip me of weapons and drag a tubular steel chair out from the side of a dining table. In seconds I'm seated in it, back against the bar, hands and feet tied to the frame, a few loops of rope around my chest and the chair back. They're not gentle, and I'm not going anywhere any time soon. Damn it, I got so close. What a waste.

From where I'm tied, I can see about half of the moon under the edge of the roof. I can see all of the circle of naked cultists. About eight or nine of them are seated in a tight circle, holding hands, chanting. The bigger gathering is forming a circle around this smaller one.

I look for my ghosts and they're near the door, all four straining forward like they're walking into a hurricane. They've made it about six feet into the room so far.

"What's holding you up?" I ask, ignoring the confused looks of the bodyguards.

"Whatever they're doing," Sly says, struggling to raise a hand to point at the smaller, seated circle. "They been at that a while now."

"Whipping up an energetic storm," Michael says.

"Fucking burns!" Graney growls.

But still they're trying to get forward. I don't know why. Get to me? Just plain curiosity? I notice Dwight doesn't say anything, but his face is twisted in concentration and he's moving farther forward than the others. He stands a little taller, seems less affected. But I don't know what difference it'll make, what can any of them do now?

"He secure?" the fat man asks over his shoulder.

"Yes, sir," one of the armed guards says.

"Then get to it! We have one minute."

The guards have a quick conversation, then one of the women stays close to me and the other five walk out onto the patio and take up ready positions. Two stand to one side, the other three move out of my line of sight toward a back corner. The waiting two hold their weapons casually, but they watch the gathering intently. Are they there to shoot someone if…what? If someone does something wrong?

"Don't know shit about shit, do you," Graney says. "Idiot."

Graney, Sly and Michael are nearer to me now, not struggling any more but leaning hard against an invisible force, seemingly just to remain in place. Their hair still whips around and the edges of them seem to stretch and fracture, like they're TV images slightly out of tune. But Dwight is still driving ahead, and he's nearly made it to the patio.

"The hell is he doing?" I ask.

"What is that idiot ever doing?" Sly asks. "I don't think even he knows."

"Like a dog barking at a squirrel because it's there, he's pushing against this shit because he can," Michael says.

The group outside join hands and start a loud chant. My ghosts make noises of pain and discomfort as the group raise their linked arms to the sky.

"Those rings they wear are combining this power somehow," Michael says, bracing harder against the preternatural wind.

Dwight yowls in angry determination, pushing harder into it. He's a couple of steps onto the patio now, his form stretching and spiking, almost breaking apart at the edges.

There's a scream and the three guards are dragging a naked, and clearly very reluctant, woman across the patio.

"NOW!" the fat man yells.

They duck under the arms of the outer ring and lift her, drop her unceremoniously into the center of the smaller circle. That group release their grips on each other and snatch from the ground glittering silver knives I hadn't noticed before. The woman tries to roll over, struggling to get up and away, but she doesn't have a chance. Those knives plunge into her, rise up, fall again. She bucks and thrashes then collapses. The larger group is chanting furiously, the woman screams as she's stabbed again and again, then her screams cease as her blood floods across the flagstones.

Even I can feel the strange wind now, a hot static that whips in eddies and vortices all around. It smells of metal and blood and something else. Something entirely unnatural. The moon expands, the half I can see growing suddenly huge, more massive than it has any right to be. Swelling from ruddy to scarlet, like the woman's blood. It blinks open like an eye.

My mind rebels at the sight, the eye staring down on the group, its iris like fire writhing in an ocean of blood. And in the center of the fire is a pupil, unfathomably huge, blacker than night, and galaxies swirl in there.

"This can't be happening," I yell, my voice whipped away by the cosmic winds. "People everywhere would see! For miles around."

"It's only happening here, in this place," Michael says, face twisted in pain. "This is outside normal space. This is impossible."

Dwight Ramsey is out there, staring up, weak, stubbled chin hanging open in shocked awe. We can only see half of it, the roof partially obscuring our view, but he's there taking in the whole profane spectacle.

"What the fuck is it?" I shout.

"Only part of it," Graney says. "That's just…a door. A gateway to something beyond, something… Fuck!"

My ghosts are staggering, clearly in pain. Dwight is shaking all over, his entire form vibrating. The cultists are chanting rhythmically, faces upturned, and I can see waves of energy washing over them, bathing them. They soak it up, gasping, exhorting, bodies flexing as it enters them. They're crying out in pain and joy. Beyond all human privilege, they gain their luck and ability, their influence, through whatever that energy is.

Even I can sense something gargantuan beyond the eye of the moon now. Some impossible entity, partially revealed, like glimpsing a whale's fin above water, knowing there's so much more of the creature out of sight. And without any prior knowledge, it's impossible to know what the rest of it might be like. Despite the energies washing down, I sense its ice-cold ambivalence. We are nothing.

Like rain washing the dirt from a road, the cloud above isn't aware of the cleaning taking place. We are insignificant. The cosmos cares not for the dust.

Luxana's words, coming back to me.

"It's incredible!" Dwight yells, and I hear him despite the now howling cosmic hurricane slamming down.

"It is vast!" Dwight says. "I can *feel* it. I could almost *touch* it! My god, y'all, it is wonderful and it is terrifying!" And he's laughing maniacally, clearly losing whatever he might have retained of his mind.

I could almost touch it!

And I remember more of Luxana talking about this thing, what she said before.

I imagine it has no idea. Their ritual simply opens something, focused through a full moon. They get the power by taking it without permission. If the entity knew, who knows what might happen? But how would it even notice?

"Dwight!" I yell into the maelstrom. "Dwight, touch it!"

"The fuck are you doing?" Graney shouts.

"Help him!" I point to Dwight. "You four, you're outside this world, this space! Bridge the gap. Get its *attention!*"

The three of them look at me for a moment, eyes wide.

"We're dead anyway, right? Otherwise?"

The three of them turn their attention to Dwight, pushing their hands forward. Dwight bucks, glances back, mouth stretched in manic laughter, then he turns his face up again. His hands shoot into the air, palms up, fingers spread wide.

"Bridge whatever unnatural space you fuckers inhabit," I scream. "Call to it!"

And Dwight starts to scream. His voice cracking, a sound beyond anything a human should be able to make, he howls through the void, shrieks into the abyss. And I feel it when the abyss hears.

Briefly, the entity out there spares Dwight a moment's thought, momentarily notices the ritual taking place. The radiation of its attention is nuclear.

The woman guarding me runs forward in shock to look, then screams at whatever she sees. She reverses her weapon and eats the barrel of her rifle, the back of her head vaporizing in the air. I'm burned, agonized, by the flood of awareness and use all my strength to launch the chair over sideways. I drive my feet against the bar to slide farther under the roof, into the corner out of view. Still I feel the unnatural searing burn of its gaze. My ghosts are screaming, their forms tattering like old rags in a gale, but still they reach, still they exhort.

But nothing overrides the screams of the gathered Acolytes of Ur. In the wash of that profane sight, they're corrupted. Thrashing and screaming, their bodies bulge and flex, they're melding into a singular mass of undulating flesh under the blasphemous awareness of whatever is out there. My ghosts are traumatized by it, but aren't physical and can't be hurt like that. Mortal flesh, it seems, has no such protection.

As the acolytes corrupt, collapsing into two rings of melded flesh, their portal ritual is interrupted. I imagine the eye of the moon snapping closed, the energies cut off. My ghosts collapse, flickering half in and half out of existence around me.

Everything seems dark and still. Looking across the floor from where I lay, I can see a massive conformation of broken flesh, weakly undulating. Dozens of people in agony, dying, but many parts not yet dead, all melted and merged, horrifically entwined. Eyes roll among hair, teeth chatter and snap, elbows and knees flex and twitch in huge rolls of skin and muscle. Moans and cries of piteous hurt and hate rise up. Coughs and mewls of horror and agony grow weaker, but don't cease.

EIGHTEEN

I T TAKES MICHAEL A PAINFUL HOUR to slowly unpick one knot at my wrist, then I can finally free myself from the rest. The whole time, that massive ring of heaving flesh moans and whimpers. The smaller circle inside is a puddle of molten skin and bone. The guards are recognizable by their clothing, but they're broken and corrupted too. Part of me wants to take my guns and end the hideous suffering, but where would I start? Are there brains behind those weakly rolling eyes? Are there organs beyond those chattering teeth? Bones poke stark and white through mounded flesh that might be one or three or ten acolytes combined. In places blood and ichor leaks across the flagstones.

Michael, Sly and Graney stay well back from it as I slowly limp around the mass. It's hideous and fascinating. Even if I could somehow end their suffering, maybe I wouldn't. Fuck these predatory assholes, every one of them. What the hell is going to happen here now? At some point, this will be found. Imagine trying to explain it. I expect it'll be covered up, an impossibility too weird to accept, so forget about it. There are a lot of victims though, the kind of people that will be missed. Not like the little people who vanish every day, who no one but their precious few really care about. It'll be interesting to see how any of the disappearances here are reported. There's not one recognizable face anywhere in this mess, so I doubt this will be realized as the final resting place of these big names, these influential people. These unnatural human predators.

Dwight is sitting cross-legged right where he was standing when it all went down. He's rocking gently, hands in his lap. As I finally come around to him, he looks up, eyes wide and manic, mouth split in a grin.

"Stronger than those fuckers, ain't I!" he says, gesturing back at the other three ghosts. "Guess maybe I might come in useful again, huh, cocheese? Better keep me around."

I can't help a laugh escaping. I guess he has a point. "You... okay?" I ask. It sounds lame.

"Fuck no, cocheese. But what choice do I have?"

I suppose that's a good point too. "Come on."

He staggers to his feet, stumbling weak but moving forward. I gather my stuff and we leave. "You two better figure out what you're good for," I say to Sly and Graney as we stumble down the stairs. "Give me good reason to keep you around as well."

NINETEEN

F OR A DAY OR TWO AFTER that horrible night I'm on edge, staying in the motel. But I don't have any of my ghosts riding on my back to hide me. No one comes after me.

Dwight is changed. It's hard to say how, exactly, but he's different. I guess time will tell just how different. If nothing else, he's quieter, which is a blessing for all of us. Even Sly is giving him a kind of side-eye of respect for what he pulled off. I guess even unrepentant, dumbass racists can grow if they're given a chance.

Back in the apartment I find most of our stuff scattered and broken, but my clothes are mostly undamaged. A few reports are coming in on the news, certain influential people missing, but it's all low key. I wonder who found what and what stories may or may not get told. I don't care, time to move on. I figure I probably won't come back to Vegas again any time soon, if at all.

My cell phone rings, the one only Bridget knows the number for. And Luxana, but I know it's not her. I already sent a text that said thanks. She was impressed, I could tell.

"Hey!" I say brightly, trying to mask the shock that still permeates me.

"Wow," Bridget says. "You're still alive." There's a palpable relief in her voice.

"Yep, against all odds, really."

"Is it over?"

"Yeah. Done. I can come to you. I don't want to be in Vegas a minute longer."

"Don't blame you. I'm not planning to come back there either."

There's a pause and I sense something in it. Some weight. My stomach sinks. "You okay?" I ask, to circle around the subject.

"I am, yeah. But Eli…" She sighs. "I'm sorry, Eli, I'm not going to tell you where I am."

Fuck. My ghosts are respectfully silent, though they watch with sad eyes. "I can't change your mind?" I ask.

"I love you, Eli. I really do. You're… Well, you're not like anyone I've ever known. I just can't deal with the weird stuff, you know? And the weird, well it's a big part of who you are, right?"

"I suppose I can't deny that. Whether I want it or not, it is."

"Yeah. I'm an earthy girl. I like the real world, I like to gamble and make money. I wish I could still do that with you, but there's more to a decision like that than I'm willing to take on."

"I get it." And I really do. I fucking hate it, but I get it. "I'm sorry, I didn't get your money back."

"I have plenty. I'm already making more. Open an account under one of your fake IDs and text me the details. I have a chunk of cash for you. You earned it, so you deserve it. I don't want to leave you struggling."

"Okay. Thanks."

"And you have this private cell number. Call if you need money or anything, yeah? Anything normal, I mean."

"I will. I love you too, Bridget. I'm sorry it had to go down this way."

"Me too. More than I can say. Take care, Eli. Try to stay out of trouble."

"You too."

There's another moment's pause, then she hangs up. I sit in stunned silence for a moment, then a text comes in.

I'm serious about the money. Please send me bank details.

I already have a couple of fake ID accounts, so I copy details from one into a text and send it. A moment later she texts:

100k deposited. Take care. xxx

Those kisses help me feel better more than the money does. Bridget is a good person, she really does deserve better than me. I text back my thanks and replicate the three kisses. Maybe one day we'll cross paths again. I hope so, but only on her terms.

With a sigh, I put the phone aside and start to redress the bullet wound in my calf. It's ugly, but my home stitching is holding. Not the first time I've patched myself up. It hurts like hell, but it's slowly getting better. As long as I don't get an infection, it should be fine.

The four ghosts are lined up along the sofa opposite me, watching in silence. I glance up at them. Michael with his head blown away on one side, Sly with his gaping chest wound, dripping blood, Graney with his throat torn open and scarlet blooms on his chest, Dwight with the pinpoint bullet hole between his newly crazed eyes. I can picture the massive exit wound that removed most of the back of his head. They look at me, half-concerned, half-expectant.

"Guess I'm on my own then," I say, with a smile. "Except for you fuckers. And all you have is me. Lucky us, eh?"

END

ABOUT ALAN BAXTER

ALAN BAXTER IS A BRITISH-AUSTRALIAN AUTHOR who writes supernatural thrillers and urban horror, rides a motorcycle and loves his dogs. He also teaches Kung Fu. He lives among dairy paddocks on the beautiful south coast of New South Wales, Australia, with his wife, son, dogs and cat. He's the multi-award-winning author of several novels and over seventy short stories and novellas. So far. Read extracts from his novels, a novella and short stories at his website – www.warriorscribe.com – or find him on Twitter @AlanBaxter and Facebook, and feel free to tell him what you think. About anything.

MORE DARK FICTION FROM
GREY MATTER PRESS

"Grey Matter Press has managed to establish itself as one of the premiere purveyors of horror fiction currently in existence."

- FANGORIA Magazine

GREY MATTER
P R E S S

CHICAGO

MANIFEST RECALL

ALAN BAXTER

"GRABS YOU BY THE NECK AND NEVER LETS GO."
— JOHN F.D. TAFF, BRAM STOKER AWARD-NOMINATED AUTHOR OF
THE END IN ALL BEGINNINGS

MANIFEST RECALL
BY ALAN BAXTER

Following a psychotic break, Eli Carver finds himself on the run, behind the wheel of a car that's not his own, and in the company of a terrified woman he doesn't know. As layers of ugly truth are peeled back and dark secrets are revealed, the duo find themselves in a struggle for survival when they unravel a mystery that pits them against the most dangerous forces in their lives.

A contemporary southern gothic thriller with frightening supernatural overtones, Alan Baxter's Manifest Recall explores the tragic life of a hitman who finds himself on the wrong side of his criminal syndicate. Baxter's adrenaline-fueled approach to storytelling draws readers into Eli Carver's downward spiral of psychosis and through the darkest realms of lost memories, human guilt and the insurmountable quest for personal redemption.

"If you like crime/noir horror hybrids, check out Alan Baxter's Manifest Recall. It's a fast, gritty, mind-f*ck." — Paul Tremblay, Bram Stoker Award-winning author of *A Head Full of Ghosts*

"*Manifest Recall* grabs you by the scruff of the neck from word one and doesn't let go. It's fast paced, bad people doing bad things to other bad people. I gobbled it down in two nights. You should, too. Highly recommended!" — John F.D. Taff Bram Stoker Award®-nominated author of *The Fearing* and *The End in All Beginnings*

GREY MATTER
P R E S S

greymatterpress.com

AN ELI CARVER SUPERNATURAL THRILLER

RECALL
NIGHT

ALAN BAXTER

"BRUTAL, GRITTY FUN..."
— BRIAN KEENE, AUTHOR OF *CITY OF THE DEAD*
AND *THE RISING*

RECALL NIGHT
BY ALAN BAXTER

Back from self-imposed exile in Canada where he fled to avoid the law following the blood-stained events in Manifest Recall—the first installment of award-winning author Alan Baxter's latest supernatural thriller series—Eli Carver returns to the states with thoughts of starting over. But an accidental encounter on a train with a mysterious woman, one he soon learns has her own dangerous past, threatens to unravel his well-intended plans.

Upon their arrival in New York, the duo quickly find themselves entangled in an ongoing war between two rival crime syndicates. And with the ghosts of his own past continuing to torment him, Eli finds himself taking the darkest of turns as he's drawn down a perilous path into a world of ancient religion and deadly occult rituals.

"Eli Carver is back with a vengeance! That's bad news for some but good news for readers. *Recall Night* is brutal, gritty fun and a phenomenal follow-up to *Manifest Recall*." — Brian Keene, author of *The Complex*

"Yet again [with *Recall Night*], Baxter has delivered an exciting story with his enigmatic protagonist at the centre, and has succeeded in whetting our appetite for more supernatural thrills in the company of Eli Carver." — *This is Horror*

GREY MATTER
P R E S S

greymatterpress.com

A COLLECTION OF CHILLING HORROR FROM AWARD-WINNING

ALAN BAXTER

"At turns creepy and visceral,
Baxter delivers the horror goods."
– Paul Tremblay, author of
The Cabin at the End of the World

SERVED
COLD

SPECIAL INTRODUCTION BY JOHN F.D. TAFF, AUTHOR OF *THE FEARING*

SERVED COLD
BY ALAN BAXTER

Collected together for the first time ever, these sixteen provocative and intensely chilling tales by multi-award-winning-author Alan Baxter venture into the depths of the darkest and most shadowy places where unspeakable horrors are the predators and we the willing prey.

Prepare for an always terrifying, frequently heartbreaking journey in multiple stages, each piece echoing Alan Baxter's unique voice that effortlessly blends horror, fantasy and the weird with elements of the dark fantastique, resulting in an unforgettable volume of fiction.

"Step into the ring with Alan Baxter, I dare you. He writes with the grace, precision, and swift brutality of a prizefighter. *Served Cold* is a stellar showcase for his talents. If you haven't had the pleasure of reading him yet, start here!" — Christopher Golden, *New York Times* bestselling author of *Ararat* and *The Pandora Room*

"In *Served Cold* Alan Baxter shows off his impressive versatility and range with a host of stories that mix old school terrors with very now concerns. At turns creepy and visceral, Baxter delivers the horror goods." — Paul Tremblay, Bram Stoker Award-winning author of *A Head Full of Ghosts* and *The Cabin at the End of the World*

"Alan Baxter's *Served Cold* is a feast for readers, who will push back from the table wanting more!" — John F.D. Taff Bram Stoker Award®-nominated author of *The Fearing* and *The End in All Beginnings*

GREY MATTER
P R E S S

greymatterpress.com

ROOSTER

A NOVEL OF ULTIMATE RETRIBUTION

AUTHOR OF THE ISLE AND MISTER WHITE

JOHN C. FOSTER

ROOSTER
by John C. Foster

John Gallo is a professional hitman with a history that's spattered in blood and littered with bodies. Known in the criminal underworld as Rooster, Gallo is an assassin suffering from mental illness and constantly battling the black dog of depression that stalks him. When able to crawl out of his downward spiral and throw himself into the job, he's a proficient, stealthy and unforgiving killer. A relentless wheeler-dealer in the game of death.

But now he finds there's a price on his head. A vendetta that could have been placed by anyone in the gangland underground. And everyone wants to collect. From two-bit street punks to the highest echelons of organized crime. The Mafia. Yakuza. Russians. Chinese. Every crime syndicate that's ever been on the bullet-end of his gun is now taking aim at him, intent on ending the reign of the Rooster.

After making a fast break from New York with a young actress rescued from certain death at the hands of the Chinese mob, Rooster is on the run and headed to his native Boston and promised refuge with his on-again, off-again criminal associate Grace. He quickly learns Beantown's dark underbelly is only interested in welcoming Rooster home so thugs and gangsters can line up to seize the prize that is his head.

Determined to solve the mystery of who wants him dead and exact his own revenge, Rooster uncovers a deadly plot with tendrils that stretch across the country, revealing a conspiracy designed to achieve the ultimate retribution.

GREY MATTER
P R E S S

greymatterpress.com

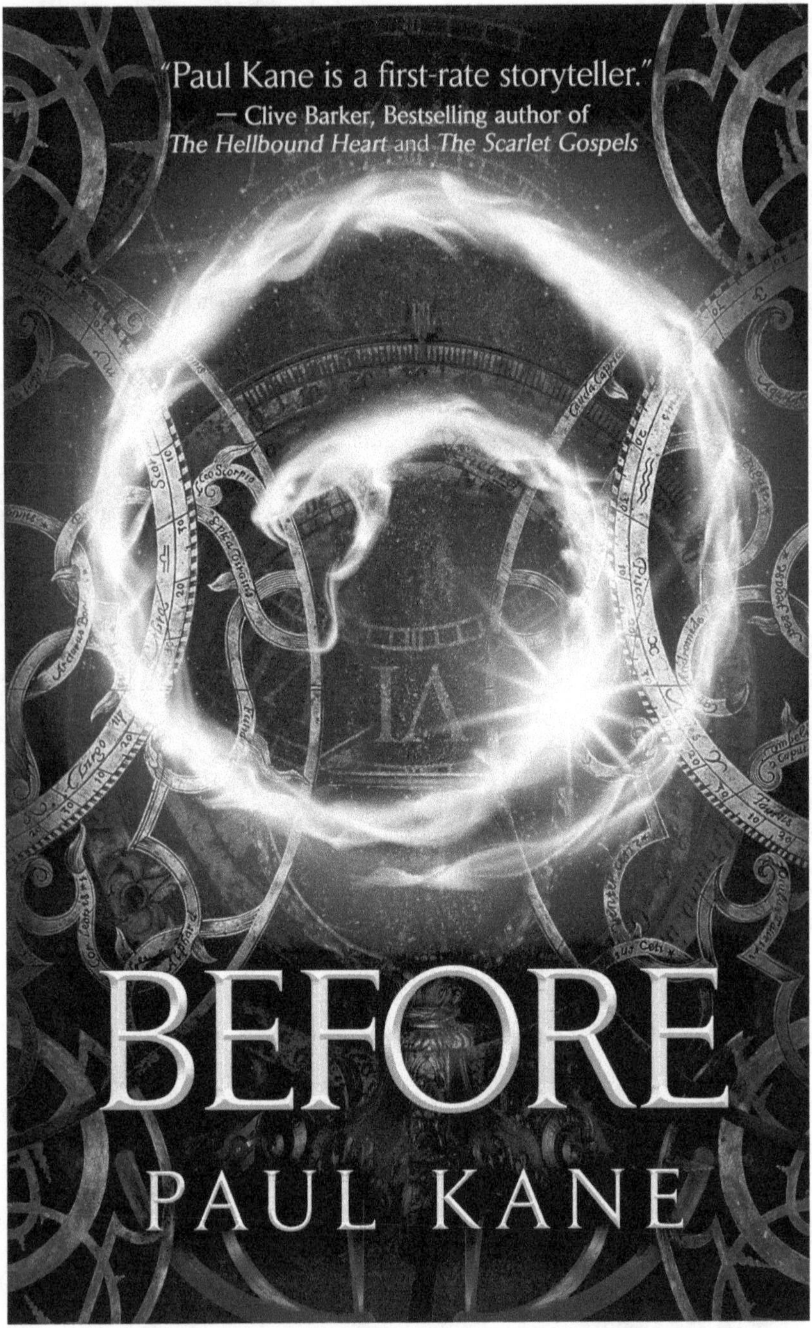
"Paul Kane is a first-rate storyteller."
— Clive Barker, Bestselling author of
The Hellbound Heart and The Scarlet Gospels
BEFORE
PAUL KANE

BEFORE
BY PAUL KANE

In 1970s Germany, a mental patient at the end of his life suddenly speaks for the first time in years. A year later in Vietnam, a mission to rescue a group of American POWs becomes a military disaster.

In present day England, the birthday of college lecturer Alex Webber sends his life spiralling out of control as a series of disturbing hallucinations lead him to the office of Dr. Ellen Hayward. And things will never be the same again for either of them. Hunted by an immortal being known only as The Infinity, their capture could mean the end of humanity itself…

Part horror story, part thrilling road adventure, part historical drama, Before is a novel like no other. Described as "the dark fantasy version of *Cloud Atlas*," Kane's *Before* is as wide in scope as it is in imagination as it tackles the greatest questions haunting mankind—Who are we? Why are we here? And where are we going?

"Paul Kane is a first-rate storyteller, never failing to marry his insights into the world and its anguish with the pleasures of phrases eloquently turned." — Clive Barker, author of *The Hellbound Heart* and *The Scarlet Gospels*

"I'm impressed by the range of Paul Kane's imagination. It seems there is no risk, no high-stakes gamble, he fears to take… Kane's foot never gets even close to the brake pedal." — Peter Straub, author of *Ghost Story*

GREY MATTER
P R E S S

greymatterpress.com

THE REAL MONSTERS ARE IN YOUR MIRROR
PEEL BACK THE SKIN
FROM BRAM STOKER AWARD® NOMINATED EDITORS
ANTHONY RIVERA
SHARON LAWSON

PEEL BACK THE SKIN
EDITED BY ANTHONY RIVERA & SHARON LAWSON

They are among us.

They live down the street. In the apartment next door. And even in our own homes.

They're the real monsters. And they stare back at us from our bathroom mirrors.

Peel Back the Skin is a powerhouse new anthology of terror that strips away the mask from the real monsters of our time – mankind.

Featuring all-new fiction from a star-studded cast of award-winning authors from the horror, dark fantasy, speculative, transgressive, extreme horror and thriller genres, *Peel Back the Skin* the work of Jonathan Maberry, Ray Garton, Tim Lebbon, Ed Kurtz, William Meikle, Yvonne Navarro, Durand Sheng Welsh, Graham Masterton, James Lowder, Lucy Taylor, Joe McKinney, Erik Williams, Charles Austin Muir, John McCallum Swain and Nancy A. Collins.

"Every single story in the book is in a class of its own. Thematically, *Peel Back the Skin* is a thing of brilliance, each story complementing or enhancing the stories around it. Top-notch, accessible and entertaining dark fiction." — Shane Douglas Keene, *This is Horror*

"Inspired and engaging. Every story is refined to a crystalline cut, their prose, their styles, their pacing and rhythms, absolutely pristine. A gradual wade out into the depths of human sub-conscious; a trawling of the blackest, most polluted realms of our collective soul." — George Daniel Lea, *The Gingernuts of Horror*

GREY MATTER
P R E S S

greymatterpress.com

AVAILABLE NOW
FROM GREY MATTER PRESS

Before — Paul Kane

The Bell Witch — John F.D. Taff

Dark Visions I — eds. Anthony Rivera & Sharon Lawson

Dark Visions II — eds. Anthony Rivera & Sharon Lawson

Death's Realm — eds. Anthony Rivera & Sharon Lawson

Devouring Dark — Alan Baxter

Dread — eds. Anthony Rivera & Sharon Lawson

The End in All Beginnings — John F.D. Taff

Equilibrium Overturned — eds. Anthony Rivera & Sharon Lawson

The Fearing (Books I-IV) — John F.D. Taff

The Fearing: The Definitive Edition — John F.D. Taff

Ghost Recall — Alan Baxter

I Can Taste the Blood — eds. John F.D. Taff & Anthony Rivera

The Isle — John C. Foster

Kill-Off — John F.D. Taff

Little Black Spots — John F.D. Taff

Little Deaths: 5th Anniversary Edition — John F.D. Taff

Manifest Recall — Alan Baxter

Mister White: The Novel — John C. Foster

The Night Marchers and Other Strange Tales — Daniel Braum

Ominous Realities — eds. Anthony Rivera & Sharon Lawson

Peel Back the Skin — eds. Anthony Rivera & Sharon Lawson

Recall Night — Alan Baxter

Rooster — John C. Foster

Savage Beasts — eds. Anthony Rivera & Sharon Lawson

Secrets of the Weird — Chad Stroup

Seeing Double — Karen Runge

Splatterlands — eds. Anthony Rivera & Sharon Lawson

Suspended in Dusk II: Anthology of Horror — ed. Simon Dewar

AN ELI CARVER SUPERNATURAL THRILLER

GHOST
RECALL

ALAN BAXTER